Neighborhood Watch

Sally Johnson

This is a work of fiction. Names, characters, organizations, places, events and incidents are either products of the author's imagination or are used fictitiously. Otherwise, any resemblance to actual persons, living or dead, is purely coincidental.

Copyright 2025 by Sally Johnson

All rights reserved.

No part of this book may be reproduced, or stored in a retrieval system, or transmitted in any form or by any means, electronic, mechanical, photocopying, recording, or otherwise, without the express written permission of the publisher.

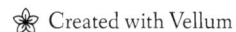

❦ Created with Vellum

Chapter 1

Perfect For Spying

The first thing I noticed when I walked into my Uncle Larry's mid-century modern house was the front window, and the perfect view of the neighbor's house directly across the street.

He stopped and nodded. "I know; it's huge."

"Perfect for spying," I said before I considered what it revealed about myself.

Larry gave me a side glance. "But it's south-facing, so it lets in a lot of sunlight. I always close the blinds in the afternoon. Otherwise, it fades the furniture."

Uncle Larry was an interior designer, so naturally he was concerned about furniture fading. My furniture was preloved IKEA and/or garage sale finds. I was more worried about my furniture *falling apart* than fading. Did laminate furniture even fade?

He removed his loafers and set them on a rack beside the door. "I never wear shoes in the house."

Even though Larry looked almost like my dad–just slightly shorter and a bit thinner–he was *very* different from my dad. My dad was laid back and Larry was meticulous—not just about his home—but his appearance as well. Every time I saw him, he was well-dressed and well-groomed. Today wasn't an exception. His dark blonde hair looked freshly cut, his face cleanly-shaven and his clothes pressed. I caught a scent of cologne–Tom Ford maybe? It was something *way* nicer than Axe.

I looked down at my outfit as I also removed my shoes. My pajama shorts and tank top were wrinkled and my "shoes" were actually UGG slippers. I caught a glimpse in the hall mirror and saw my tangle of long, brown hair was escaping from my messy bun. I quickly looked away. It reflected the truth–that I had just literally rolled out of bed, hopped on a train and slept most of the trip from Connecticut.

Before I could place my shoes on the rack, Bojangles, his mini Jack Russell terrier, bounded in. He barked at me as if he was really vicious.

"Attack!" Larry joked.

Bojangles was too busy sniffing my shoes to take a bite out of me.

"Give him a minute and you'll be his new best friend," he said.

"I hope so." We'd be spending the next week together. Which was one of the reasons why I was there: dog-sitting.

"Bojangles, meet Isla. Isla, meet Bojangles."

I knelt down, offered a fist for him to smell before I reached out and gave him a tenuous pat on the head. "Hello, Bojangles."

The dog rolled over and showed me his belly, which I took as a good sign.

After a few minutes of playing with Bojangles, Larry gave me a tour. It was a one-story house that had the traditional hallmarks of the mid-century modern style. The open floor plan consisted of the living room opening into the kitchen and dining area on the east side of the house. Wood beams on the ceiling were made of the same wood as the built-in buffet in the dining room and the accent wall in the living room. The three bedrooms were down a hallway off of the living room. Each room was furnished in sleek furniture made of teak and his whole house smelled of lemons. I assumed it was from furniture polish since everything looked shiny and new. Unlike my two-bedroom apartment that was, aside from the previously mentioned used furniture, on the dull and dusty side.

Larry walked me to the guest bedroom, which was also west-facing. The sun was setting, but still shone boldly through the window. I hoped there were blackout shades or I'd have to find another room to sleep in.

"My doctor told me to rest in a dim room for at least twelve hours a day," I said. Articulating how much time I was supposed to do nothing but rest overwhelmed me. That was *all day*.

"Then this *obviously* won't work." He nodded, understanding the problem. "It'll have to be the master bedroom then."

In one succinct movement, he wheeled my hard-shell carry-on suitcase over the oak floor and across the hall. The room was double the size of the guest room, a king size bed and complete with an en-suite bathroom. Even though it'd just be me and Bojangles for the week, it made me feel a little more bougie to be upgraded to the nicer room.

As we circled back by the front door, Larry pointed to the wall. "I recently installed the security system and also the doorbell camera. Unfortunately, I haven't taken the time to tweak the settings on the doorbell and the motion detection feature is sensitive. I hope it's not too disruptive."

"What do you mean by sensitive?" I imagined a "disruptive" doorbell ringing all the time.

"It picks up motion as far as the end of the driveway and chimes. Two days ago a cat walked across the driveway with a rat in its mouth. I don't need to be alerted every time a cat walks across my property or headlights flash in my driveway. And now I have to worry that they," he nodded across the street, "have rats." He sighed heavily.

"Is there a lot of crime in the neighborhood?" I asked, glancing back out the front window. *Or rats? Gag!*

Larry lived in one of those towns in Massachusetts that was spelled one way and pronounced another. The town didn't seem to be a rough area. Most of the houses I had seen driving with him had been traditional Capes and split-level houses from the eighties. But Larry's neighborhood was a cluster of similar style homes on a quiet cul-de-sac. There were three houses on each side of the street and they all looked well-kept, except for the one directly across from Larry's. It looked like it belonged in a rough part of a city instead of a tranquil suburban neighborhood. It was a small, rundown fortress with bars on the windows and doors, junk in the yard and overgrown trees.

"There's been a rash of catalytic converter thefts, and our police department is short-staffed because of budget cuts. It's a shame, but it is what it is." He shrugged. "They have more serious calls to respond to, so stolen car parts aren't their priority. But I'm not too worried about someone breaking in or stealing my catalytic converter. It's a very quiet neighborhood and I always park in the garage."

He had picked me up from the train station in his BMW SUV. I, obviously, would also park in the garage because I wouldn't want anything to happen to his beloved car or his catalytic converter on my watch. He definitely paid more money for that vehicle than I made in a year as a claims processor. There was no way I could afford to replace anything on that car and I certainly didn't want all my dog-sitting money to be used to buy a new catalytic converter.

We moved into the kitchen, which, like the rest of his house, was sleek, minimalist and warm wood tones. He pointed out the doggy door for Bojangles and a plastic cover. "I close the door at night."

"How come?"

"Wild animals occasionally wander through the yard. Sometimes we get coyotes or raccoons. I don't want them attacking Bojangles and I definitely don't want them inviting themselves in. Poor baby would be so scared if he went missing in the dark. So if he needs to go out after 9 p.m., I always go with him."

I gulped at the thought of a raccoon randomly wandering in through the doggy door. You think they're super cute with those sad eyes and little hands until they attack you and give you rabies. "Okay," I said, making a mental note.

"This is the basement door," he said, pointing beside the fridge. "You shouldn't have any reason to go down there."

I shivered. I wasn't a big fan of basements anyway. "Is it finished?" I pictured dirt floors, low ceilings and lots of spiders. Sort of like my grandma's.

"Sadly, no. It's still in its 1960's glory." He shimmied his hands. "It needs a complete reno and is a big project and one I don't have time for right now. So I ignore it."

If Larry ignored it, I'd ignore it.

Larry pushed a small binder and a file folder across the

marble counter toward me. Inside the folder was a sheet labeled "Living at Larry's". I gave it a cursory glance. Everything he had told me was neatly typed out on linen stationery.

He tapped the paper. "Here's what we've gone over. And some other important things like the phone number for the neighbor to my right and the non-emergency number for the police."

"Okay." I was pretty sure I wouldn't need any of those. This was going to be a quiet, uneventful week that would most likely be boring.

"My cleaning girl, Annie, comes on Thursday. As long as you keep up with the dishes, she'll handle the rest."

It was almost like staying at a hotel. "Great."

"I also included the garage code, the house alarm code and instructions on how to use the TV. I have *all* the channels, although I don't know why. I hardly ever watch them."

Which would have been very important if I *could* watch TV. My doctor had given me strict instructions to limit my total screen time to sixty to ninety minutes a day.

While he did a quick inventory of available foods I could "help myself to", I skimmed the paper which included a list of daily chores such as getting the mail and watering the plants. There was a completely separate *binder* for Bojangles.

It listed the phone number for the vet, feeding times, walk times and tidbits like: *I never, ever let him off leash! He's not a runner unless he gets spooked.*

He opened a vintage teak cabinet that had several framed pictures of Bojangles on top of it. "This is my bar," he said and launched into very specific guidelines about it. "Be careful with this door because sometimes it sticks." He demonstrated opening a cabinet door that stored vintage etched highball glasses. "If I entertained more, maybe that hinge wouldn't be so cranky."

I definitely wouldn't be doing *any* entertaining. "Don't worry," I reassured him. "I was told absolutely no drinking while I'm recovering."

We moved back into the front room. "How is the concussion anyway? I can't believe a slip-and-fall has such a long recovery. That just blows my mind." He made an explosion motion and sound.

I couldn't believe it, either. The injury would've been less serious and recovery would've been quicker if I had just gone to the hospital after I slipped on the kitchen floor, hit my head on the granite island going down, and landed on the tile floor. It seemed ridiculous (at the time) to go to the hospital for a bump on the head. It was embarrassing to admit I had literally slipped in spilled milk. Since then, I had cried over spilled milk, because of it and my fall, I was now put on "head rest" so I could recover. "It's going to be slow-going. I'm prescribed rest, darkness, and not too much stimulation. I have to wear a hat and sunglasses whenever I go outside. If all goes well, I should be fully recovered in a year."

Saying the words out loud made me want to cry inside. I was only two weeks into my recovery and fifty more weeks was so long! I suffered from sensitivity to light and sound, confusion, brain fog, slow reaction time when driving because it took longer to process things, migraines and insomnia. It was the perfect storm for boredom and depression.

I hoped that my week-long stay here would be a needed change of pace and maybe even a nice distraction.

Larry demonstrated which remotes worked for what in

the front room–including electronics and the dark, automatic shades.

"Thanks again for doing this," he said as he put down the remote for the shades, leaving the curtains open about two feet so the room didn't go completely dark. "You just don't know who you can trust these days." He scooped Bojangles up and kissed him. "Especially when it comes to taking care of my Bojangles," he said in a lovey-dovey voice.

I shrugged. "You're actually helping me. It's not like I can do anything else right now. " Technically, I couldn't work and might not be able to for months. I didn't miss working–processing insurance claims was monotonous–but I missed spending time with co-workers. House- and dog-sitting for Larry was an easy way to make a little extra money until my short-term disability kicked in. And, hey, who didn't love hanging out with an adorable dog?

He glanced at his watch. "I have an Uber scheduled to pick me up soon. Do you have any questions about anything?"

I shook my head. "Not that I can think of."

"If you do, just call. If I don't pick up, I'll call you back as soon as I can. Unless I'm in a conversation with someone *truly* boring–then I'll gladly take your call. Sometimes at the social events you get stuck talking to a wind bag."

I laughed at his brutal honesty. I wasn't worried. He had explained everything and left the detailed instructions sheet. All I had to do was make sure the house didn't burn down and his dog didn't get injured or die. It was all pretty straight-forward.

A chime from his doorbell camera floated through the air and Larry glanced out the window. "There's the annoying chime," he said and gave me a fake smile. "My

Uber awaits. I'll call tonight and check on how things are going."

"We'll be great," I said confidently before he closed the front door. He climbed into his Uber and was off to catch his flight to New York City for a decorators convention.

I glanced at Bojangles and he cocked his head at me. He didn't seem worried. I mean, really, what could go wrong?

Chapter 2

What Was the Deal With the Neighbors?

I plopped onto the gray couch, which was firm and scratchy. It was probably very expensive, but it felt like sitting on a wooden box. Bojangles jumped up beside me.

"Bojangles," I said to my furry companion. His head cocked in recognition of his name. "I'm not sure if you're allowed on the furniture, but I won't tell if you won't tell."

He settled down. I knew we'd get along just fine for the next week.

I scanned the room, wondering if any of the other seating was more comfortable. There was a wingback chair that was extremely upright and looked to be the same material as the couch. I guessed it wasn't just the fabric that was similar. I tried the seat just in case. It was as uncomfortable as expected.

In the corner of the room, beside a rubber tree plant that reached the top of the eight-foot ceiling, was a sleek, reclining, leather seat with a wooden frame. I tentatively sat down on it. It was pleasantly comfortable. In fact, it was amazing! I reclined a little, which resulted in reclining all the way.

Neighborhood Watch

The more reclined the chair, the more I liked it. It was so comfortable I could see myself spending many of my nine hours of mandatory headrest in it.

Bojangles jumped up on my lap and snuggled in. Having nothing better to do, since my screen time was limited as was my noise exposure and light exposure, I cued up an episode of my favorite true crime podcast, *What the Heck?!*. I hadn't used my whole allotment of "listening time" for the day and this was the perfect way to relax. Then I shimmied out of my pants, dropped them on the floor and reclined. I put my phone on my Do Not Disturb, put in my AirPods and closed my eyes. I was so tired from traveling. Within minutes, I dozed off.

* * *

The chime from the motion sensor woke me. Bojangles immediately started barking. Even if I could sleep through the chime, I couldn't sleep through the barking. I opened my eyes and saw lights shining through the gap in the curtains. Confused and groggy, I struggled to recognize my surroundings. An eerie figure in the corner came into focus as my eyes adjusted to the darkness and turned out to be the rubber plant. It took me a moment to remember I was at Larry's. Off in the distance, I thought I heard dogs barking. How long had I been asleep? I glanced at my watch. 1:18 a.m.

I rubbed my eyes and shifted my legs. Bojangles was sprawled across them and not willing to move. Forcing the reluctant dog out of his spot, I swung my feet off the chair. My toes hit something and my phone skittered across the floor. I vaguely recall turning on the podcast and realized my phone must've fallen off my lap while I was asleep. I retrieved it and swiped up on the screen. There was one missed call from Larry, but I couldn't call him back at this hour and the battery was almost dead. I tried to remember where exactly I had packed the charger. Guessing it was in my purse or my carry-on, I went to get it.

Not wanting to disturb the darkness or shock my eyes any more than necessary, I didn't turn on the lights. They would only strain my eyes, and thus make my head hurt.

Bojangles followed me as I headed for the bedroom, but stopped at the front door and began frantically barking. Crap! He hadn't been out since I'd gotten there. Despite the doggie door in the kitchen, it was definitely after 9 p.m. And Bojangles needed to be walked morning and night. Did one in the morning count for both morning and night?

"Give me a second, puppy," I called from the bedroom as I dug through the many pockets of my bag until my fingers touched the fiber cord. I hurried back to the front room, where Bojangles now jumped and yapped at the door. Last thing I needed was for him to have an accident on my uncle's beautiful wood floors. And I definitely didn't want to pick up a steaming pile of dog poop. Just the thought of it made me gag.

Plugging in my phone would have to wait.

I looked around the entryway, trying to remember where Larry told me the harness and leash were. I found the leash coiled neatly on the top of the shoe rack. As for the harness—it was nowhere to be found. Nothing was hanging on hooks. There wasn't a basket near the shoe rack. And I still wasn't willing to disturb my head by turning on the lights.

As Bojangles' barks became more frenzied, combined with running in circles, I made a split-second decision to skip the harness. Just this one time. After all, it was the middle of the night. And Bojangles was trained. He probably could go without a leash and be fine. I doubted he would get spooked and run off at this hour, but just in case he tried, I put the leash on. That would have to be good enough.

I stepped out into the stillness of the midnight air, quietly clicking the front door shut. The night was quiet, and I didn't want to disturb the peace, so I tiptoed across the cool concrete porch. It was chilly despite it being early summer. And, in my haste, I forgot I was only wearing a t-shirt—no shorts or shoes. I decided to not go back in because it wasn't like anybody would see me. Who else was up at this hour of the night?

Slam!

A car door shut. Then another. The sound shattered the silence.

I looked in the direction the noise came from and realized it was the neighbors across the street.

Instinctively, I stepped back. Oh crap! What if they could see I was pantsless?

What were they doing up?

Were they getting home from work or a late night out?

With the dim illumination the street lights provided, I could make out movement in the driveway.

I moved farther back into the shadow of the front porch.

The trunk popped open, lighting up the small cavity. The man retrieved what looked like a dark bag from the trunk while the woman waited beside him.

Bojangles let out a low growl.

"Shh! Shh!" I said, squatting down beside Bojangles to comfort him. I didn't want the neighbors to know we were out there. I didn't know why. What if I surprised them? Or worse, scared them? What if they carried a concealed weapon, perceived me as a threat and shot me?

Maybe I'd been listening to too many true-crime podcasts.

I sat on the cold, concrete step of the porch and let Bojangles have the length of the leash to sniff around the bushes. I held my breath as I watched the neighbors, just in case they could somehow hear me breathe or feel my presence.

What was with my paranoia?

From my perch on the porch, I observed what looked like boxes being unpacked and brought into the house. They moved steadily back and forth from the car to the house–the man doing the lifting and the woman seemingly directing his actions. Or, that was my best guess. I could hear bits and pieces of a conversation, but couldn't decipher much. It went on for about five minutes. When the final box had been delivered into the house, the man slammed the trunk.

Bojangles barked; his reaction rang through the night air.

Their heads swiveled in my direction.

I leaned back farther, hoping they wouldn't locate me. The woman walked to the side of the man. Both of them looked around—to the left and to the right—and then finally across the street.

Right at me.

I guessed my presence was given away when the couple approached the end of the driveway. In the dim, yellow light of the streetlight, I could see they were older. Surely, that meant they were harmless, right?

I stood, stepped forward and waved, trying to ease the awkward feeling that I got caught doing something wrong.

Neighborhood Watch

In reality, though, I only got caught walking the dog in my t-shirt and underwear. Was that a crime? Maybe in the daylight. But certainly not at night when one could hardly see me.

Yet, they stood there and stared at me. Even though I couldn't confirm it, I was pretty sure they also gave me a nasty look.

"Nice night, huh?" I called out to break the ice. It only further sliced through the stillness of the night.

"Mind your business," the woman called. The couple hurried up the driveway and slammed the front gate with a loud *clang!*. The car lock beeped and the front door banged shut behind them.

Wounded, I tried to soothe my hurt feelings. "What's their problem?" I said to Bojangles. "I was just trying to be friendly." He didn't respond, of course, but instead lifted his leg and marked a bush. I hurried him along by wiggling his leash and offering words of encouragement. "C'mon, buddy. Poop! You can do it. I know you can."

Bojangles lingered around the bushes for a few minutes, sniffing, marking his territory, but never actually doing any business serious enough to warrant a midnight walk. After giving him one, two, three more warnings, I finally guided him inside.

Back in the safety of Larry's home, I returned to my now-favorite chair.

"What happened?" I asked Bojangles, trying to process the experience. Was it just weird trying to be social in the dark at that time in the morning? Had I startled them? Or were they just unfriendly people? Those were the only excuses I could come up with.

Bojangles jumped on my lap to comfort me.

A slice of light from their house caught my attention. It

was such a stark contrast to the darkness, it was hard *not* to notice. And after what just went down, I was curious.

I leaned forward on the chair to get a better view through the window, careful to remain hidden behind the safety of the curtains.

Their floor plan must've been a mirror image of my uncle's house because they also had the large front window. Their curtains were thick enough to provide privacy, but a curtain flipped, which provided a small glimpse into the front room. Or, at least what I could see from the gap that was not closed by curtains. The little bit I could see revealed the man as he stacked a box on top of an already-large pile of boxes next to a similar pile of boxes. Had they just moved in?

Needing a better look, I wrestled the chair across the floor, half-carrying half-dragging (being very careful not to scrape the floor) it closer to the window. My determination was fueled by a combination of curiosity, boredom and a lack of stimulation. I had sunk so low that I was now spying on strangers. I was ashamed to admit this had been the most entertainment I'd had all day.

Barely a few seconds later, the woman marched to the window, looked to the left and to the right and seemingly stared straight across at me, then snapped the curtains shut.

What was the deal with those neighbors?

Chapter 3
Turns Out, Head Rest is Boring

I slept in the chair the rest of the night, Bojangles still nestled between my knees. When I awoke, the dull pain of a headache pulled at my temples, or maybe remained. The middle-of-the-night excitement left me feeling tired and off-kilter. It was so odd—the whole interaction with the neighbors, their behavior, their movements.

I replayed the strange encounter in my mind as I ate a bowl of Cheerios and fed Bojangles his breakfast. Knowing we'd be going out for a morning walk would give me a chance to get a better look. Now that I needed to know more about them, I was interested in checking out their property.

Gearing up for Bojangles' walk took a lot more preparation for me than it did for him. He just needed a leash, a harness (which I still couldn't find) and a poop bag. Me–I needed a hat and hideous, wrap-around sunglasses. You know–the kind old people wear *over* their normal glasses when they're driving their RVs. The big, dark ones with the side panels that go almost to your ears. Yeah, those.

But the sacrifice of fashion was worth it just to get a

better look at the house across the street. When I took the dog out for his morning walk (still sans harness), I paid close attention to the neighbor's house.

It was a one-story house like Larry's, but a dull, dingy white color. Security bars cased the windows and enclosed the front porch, and a metal gate prevented entry to the front door. It reminded me of a jail cell. The right side of the house had an attached garage and beside that, another metal gate similar to the one on the front door. A tall wooden fence started at the far left corner of the house, and extended to what I assumed was the property line. Several "NO TRESPASSING" signs were posted on it. High boxwood shrubs ran along the length of the wooden fence, with smaller rose bushes in front of them creating a two-deep line of defense. More rose bushes were randomly planted around the shrubs and in the yard, accented with faded pink flamingos stuck into the ground by metal stakes. It looked unkempt instead of manicured and aesthetically pleasing. From the length of the grass to the overgrowth of bushes, it was obvious it'd been a while since their landscaper had visited.

Square, Home Depot moving boxes were stacked on the front patio up to the edge of the windowsill. Were they moving? That might explain what they were doing last night. But there wasn't a For Sale sign in the yard. And they couldn't possibly be moving in–everything in the yard looked like it had been there for years–old, faded and becoming one with the surroundings.

Beside the boxes and next to the door was a three-tier metal shelf that had crumbling plastic planters filled with bunches of dull, fake flowers. A garland of silk fall leaves hung around the door frame and a second garland hung on the entryway gate. At the threshold of the door was a giant frog planter.

In the driveway was an old, faded, yellow Mustang parked in front of the garage. One of the back tires was flat, so it was safe to assume it wasn't driven anymore. To the side, on what should've been part of the lawn, was a faded metal bench, a blue tarp covering what looked to be some sort of metal hoist. Beside that, a stack of tires and a rusty motorcycle missing the handlebars. There was a folded-up treadmill; the base was covered in a mound of dead leaves. Backed up in front of the Mustang, was the car they drove last night–a newer, bumblebee yellow SUV that looked to be in decent shape.

From the outside, the house was still. The curtains were tightly drawn on the front window and every other window I could see. The garage had those tiny top panel windows, but they were covered up with tin foil.

As I meandered through the neighborhood, I made some mental observations. Most of the houses I walked by had mowed lawns and flower gardens. Some had an American flag hanging from the porch and a white, picket fence. Despite the usual clutter of notices stapled to the telephone poles looking for missing pets or advertising yard sales, the area Larry lived in seemed pretty nice. And it served as a glaring contrast to the look and feel of the neighbor's house.

By the end of the walk, I wasn't any closer to understanding last night's incident. Maybe the people that lived in that house were like my grandma who had passed. She was old and just had a lot of stuff.

I gave up trying to make any sense of it and wrote the neighbors off as weirdos. With nothing else to do, and feeling mentally fatigued, I took a pill to stave off the headache and settled in my new favorite chair for my first morning nap.

* * *

After a short rest (I never actually fell asleep–I was too busy reviewing the events of the last twenty-four hours), I called Larry. I glanced at the clock, realizing I hadn't even checked before I hit "dial". 11:30 a.m. There was a chance I'd catch him going to lunch.

"Hi, Isla," he said when he picked up.

I put him on speaker, and Bojangles' ears perked up at the sound of Larry's voice.

"Hey. Sorry I didn't answer last night. I fell asleep and slept through your call."

"I figured it was something like that. How is everything going?"

"Good," I said.

"How are you and Bojangles getting along?" he asked.

I petted the dog's head. "Practically best friends at this point."

"Bojangles is like that. He's my good dog."

With the small talk over, it was time to finally get to what I really wanted to know. "What's the deal with the older couple across the street?"

"Ohhhhhhh, yes. The Miltons. Mildred and Glen."

"I woke up in the middle of the night and they were in their driveway unloading stuff from their car. Are they moving in? Or out?"

"Nooo. They've been there for years. I wish they would move." I could almost *hear* Larry's eyes roll. "They are a blight to the neighborhood."

Blight was right. "It was so strange."

"They're strange. Mildred reminds me of the witch in Hansel and Gretel and it's not just because of her crazy hair. I'm pretty sure she has an oven in her backyard to burn trespassers."

I gulped. "Really?"

"Once I helped Glen move a large generator back there. That's when I saw it."

"Did you ask about it?"

"Of course! I couldn't *not* ask!"

"Well?" I demanded, my curiosity piqued. "What did he say?"

"He claimed it was for pizza," Larry said.

"Did you believe him?"

"They've never invited me over for pizza. Or brought me pizza. It has never even *smelled* like they were baking pizza in their backyard."

"But you said it was an oven."

"It was like a brick oven-type thing. It was the worst DIY I'd ever seen," Larry said, the disdain evident in his voice.

By the look of their yard, they didn't look like meticulous people.

"Have you ever seen them up in the middle of the night?" Larry hadn't answered the question that my inquiring mind wanted to know: *what* were they doing?

"I sleep like a rock," he said. "I guess there's alway the possibility that they're squirrel trappers or collect roadkill to taxidermy."

Squirrel trappers? Roadkill taxidermy? Gross! Is that really what he thought his neighbors did?

He continued. "But honestly, I like my sleep too much to care."

Which is probably what I should try to do–care about

my sleep and *not* care about the neighbors.

The chime of the bell, the roar of a diesel engine and the barks of Bojangles interrupted our conversation as a UPS truck pulled in front of the Milton's. I said goodbye to Larry and turned my attention to the view from the front window. I watched, more bored than curious, to see what sort of things they ordered. Were they Amazon shoppers (but that would've been an Amazon truck), QVC or Home Shopping Network shoppers or maybe just good ol' Target?

From where I was, I couldn't see much. The body of the truck blocked most of my view. I did see several large, flat boxes on a hand truck, but was unable to see if the boxes had logos on them.

As the truck turned around and drove past Larry's driveway, the motion detector chimed. Bojangles reacted to the noise with obligatory barking. Larry was right, the doorbell/motion chime was a little too sensitive and becoming annoying.

I closed the shades, put in my ear plugs, put on my eye mask and reclined the chair for my next mandatory rest.

* * *

A sense of déjà vu hit me when I awoke; I was back in the chair, Bojangles was back in the nook of my knees, things were the same as when I fell asleep. I was in the exact same position and the rubber tree hadn't branched out in any visible, noticeable way. The only difference was the headache had subsided.

I sighed.

I got up, got a glass of water, made a sandwich and looked around in an attempt to decide what to do. Nothing! I could do nothing! I was supposed to rest. And that was it.

I switched rooms. Maybe a change in "scenery" would help me relax and settle down. Larry's king size bed was very comfortable, the room darker, but it didn't alleviate the boredom and the looming case of mild, situational depression.

I checked my phone. My roommate, Sierra, finally responded to my text I had sent when I had arrived.

Sierra: How are you feeling?

Me: Other than the concussion, fine. Are you sick?

Sierra: Yeah. Probably just the flu.

Now I was glad I wasn't home to catch it.

Me: Feel better.

I sent a few other texts. I didn't expect to have immediate responses to, but surprisingly did.

Lola: We're in sexual harassment training for the next two days. ☹

Lola was my bestie from work. Lately it had been hard to add much to our conversations when she was the only one with news. I might've dodged a boring work training, but HR would eventually catch up to me and make sure I completed the mandatory requirements.

Me: Enjoy! LOL!

I clicked on the text from my mom and scrolled through the photos she had sent, but stopped after two.

I dropped my phone on the comforter and resisted the urge to keep scrolling through social media. I had forgotten to bring my blue light blocking glasses which allowed me precious screen time. Since they were an absolute necessity, I needed to have a pair here. If I ordered them now, I could hopefully have them by tomorrow and it would give me something to look forward to.

Sally Johnson

I pulled up the Amazon app and quickly ordered a pair, with guaranteed next-day delivery straight to my uncle's house. My hopes soared. I could do a mini-binge watch of a show—any show—to add variety to my day. If my current life was a reality TV show, viewers would see nothing but me flopping around on the bed. Five minutes on my stomach, ten on my back, then some on my side, only to roll over to the other side. It was a steady flow of changing position, not just trying to get comfortable, but to alleviate my restlessness.

But even when I had my blue light glasses and eventually found a comfy position, it would not cure my biggest temptation to scroll on my phone: the fear of missing out.

Yes, I had a bad case of FOMO.

See, while I was here at my uncle's house, the rest of my immediate family and most of my mom's side, was at my cousin's wedding. A destination wedding. On a cruise. To the Caribbean.

I had done everything I could to convince my parents and my doctor that I was healthy enough to go. My parents overrode me, despite my being twenty-five and old enough to make my own decision, because they had paid for the cruise. They deferred to the doctor's recommendation, but my doctor couldn't be swayed. He said I shouldn't travel or have that amount of constant stimulation. Despite promises to rest, bribe attempts, deals and bargains, I wasn't able to convince my doctor to clear me for the trip. I was able to get a credit for the part of the trip I'd paid for (the plane ticket), but it did little to soothe my feelings of missing out.

Instead of enjoying the beaches and sunsets of the Caribbean, the festivities and most importantly, the wedding, I was here. Stuck. Resting on a bed in a dark room all day, every day. It sucked.

I could text family members on the cruise, but I knew the schedule was busy. Would they really want to take time out of their vacation/wedding experience to update on all the happenings in real time? No. I wouldn't want to have to do that for someone not attending. And no one wanted to be constantly bothered by my texts while they were on vacation and away from cellular service while at sea. What would my texts read anyway? *I'm bored. I have nothing to do. Just took a nap. Ate lunch. Going to take another nap.* It would take a concerted effort not to sink into a deep depression.

I could text Lola again, but she was working. I doubted anything had happened in the last five minutes.

I wasn't just bored–I was lonely too. I didn't have a serious boyfriend or anyone I'd dated more than one or two times. It just hadn't clicked.

Everyone had something to do–whether it was working or traveling.

My options for entertainment were, as previously stated, limited and I mentally searched for alternate options. I settled on listening to another true-crime podcast, then tried to take another nap, only to give up and go look for a snack.

After eating, I took a lap around the interior of the house, to get in a few steps that I could call light exercise and then accepted the harsh reality that it was time for another nap.

My life was like my own personal version of the movie *Groundhog Day*.

And the next day would be exactly like the day before.

It turns out head rest is boring.

Head rest, like the common practice of pregnant

women prescribed bed rest, is exactly what it sounds like. It is resting my brain from all stimulation.

I had a sister-in-law who had been put on bedrest when she was six months pregnant. She said it was horrible. She was supposed to stay in bed all day except getting up to use the bathroom or get a meal. At the time, I was eighteen and working full-time at a retail job I hated and being put on bedrest sounded wonderful. Nothing sounded more fun than being told I *had* to stay in bed *all* day long.

Even now, at twenty-five, laying around, doing nothing, sounded ideal—at first.

Originally, not having to get dressed or go to work was a dream-come-true treatment for a concussion until I actually had to take my dose of "medicine". The doctor had prescribed twelve weeks of this. After twelve weeks of "intensive" head rest, I could transition to "moderate" head rest and finally "light" head rest. The prospect of more activity was exciting, but the time periods were not hard and fast and could change according to doctor's orders. I was only two weeks in. Last week wasn't so bad. I basked in the thoughts of the glorious amount of time I had off, the naps, the excitement of house-sitting for Uncle Larry and the obscene amount of money he was paying me to watch his dog (1st priority) and his house too (2nd priority). But now…here I was…and at a loss.

I looked around. I had nothing to do, nor could I do anything I *wanted* to do. I couldn't binge-watch my favorite shows or catch up on missed seasons or even experience my cousin's wedding vicariously through social media until my blue light glasses came. Because I had listened to the podcast, my "outside stimulation" was used up. Music was out. Reading was out. Audio books were out. Sunlight and exposure to sun was limited.

I could text someone...if they weren't all on the trip or working.

I could go back to bed...but I wasn't tired.

I could take the dog for a walk...but at sunset...and it was barely afternoon.

I was so wrong! Head rest wasn't fun at all.

Chapter 4

What If the Dog On the Other Side of the Fence Was In Heat?

After a long day of literally doing nothing, twilight finally descended and, at last, it was time to take Bojangles for a walk. The harness had eventually been located in a basket labeled "Bojangles" in the laundry room and had been the result of a boredom-induced search, in which I also peeked in closets, opened bathroom mirror cabinets and checked out what was stored in my uncle's (very neat and organized) garage.

"How does this work?" I asked the dog. It was some fancy sort of contraption that had so many clips and adjustments that I couldn't figure it out.

He provided no response.

"Never mind," I muttered to myself. "You can't talk. You're a dog." Although I kind of wished he could respond. Imagine the conversations we could have. It would definitely make things less boring.

I held it up, flipped it around, flipped it around again, and finally set in on the floor. I wrangled Bojangles' legs through the straps, only to discover the clips didn't line up.

Seriously?

Neighborhood Watch

After a few more attempts at the harness, I gave up. It was not for a lack of trying. I'd get it on one way, only to have the clips not line up. Or realize it was backwards. Or upside down. Or something wasn't right. Figuring it out literally made my head hurt. Bojangles could survive *one* walk with the leash clipped to his collar. When I wasn't so desperate to leave the house, I'd take the time to figure out the intricacies of the harness.

The walk around the block turned into twice around the block and was the best walk I'd ever taken in my whole entire life.

As we entered the cul-de-sac and approached the odd neighbors' house, a dog barked from behind their fence, followed by a menacing growl. *They have a dog?* I thought I'd heard dogs barking off in the distance last night, but didn't realize it was directly across the street. I stepped off the curb and turned right toward Larry's house.

Bojangles had other plans.

He pulled left, growling and barking, toward the unknown enemy on the other side of the fence, and slipped out of his collar.

"Bojangles!" I cried, holding the limp leash.

He sprinted across the lawn and behind a large, overgrown rose bush, then into the thick Boxwood hedge that hid most of the wooden fence.

Crap! Where'd he go?

I started after him.

"Bojangles?" I called in a fierce whisper as I approached the fortress of shrubbery. "Here, boy! Come, boy!" I tiptoed forward and peeked around, trying to see if he was anyplace obvious. I prayed I'd catch sight of him, grab him and run away. No harm, no foul.

No Bojangles.

Wait! What is that?

I could hear something.

Was that him?

I heard...movement. Panting. Scratching.

Oh, gosh! Bojangles was fixed, wasn't he?

What if the dog on the other side of the fence was in heat?

Horror washed over me at the idea of Bojangles becoming a puppy-daddy. That'd be on me. Larry would be so disappointed. And how would the weird neighbors react?

I dropped to my hands and knees and crawled around the edge of the landscaping. I looked as best I could under the rose bushes, but it was difficult. "Ouch! Ow!" I cursed as I pushed branches out of my way. The thorns had no compassion for my plight. "Bojangles," I called, my voice taking on a pleading tone.

Please, please don't impregnate the neighbors' dog. Please!

"Bark! Bark! Bark!"

Was that him? I couldn't identify if it was Bojangles' bark, or the dog behind the fence. "Bojangles!" I hissed. The last thing I wanted was a confrontation with the unfriendly neighbors and be accused of being a Peeping Tom, or more accurately, a Peeping Isla.

I systematically checked the row of bushes, carefully pulling them away from the fence to look behind them. I could still *hear* the dogs, I just couldn't *see* them.

At the very corner of the fence, there was a fresh mound of dirt. A hole had been dug just big enough for Bojangles to squeeze under. Even if I pressed my face flat against the ground, I could barely see anything.

"Dang it!" I stood, wiped the dirt off and steeled myself for what I had to do next.

My heart thudded with every step as I approached the front door.

They could be really nice people.

Maybe I had caught them at a bad moment last night and that's not how they really are. Or maybe they were worried about being approached by a stranger in the middle of the night. Although I doubted I looked menacing in a T-shirt and underwear.

Maybe they'll be friendly.

Maybe some of that would be true if I could ring the doorbell–only it was on the other side of the gate. How in the world would I reach it? Why have a doorbell if no one could reach it? It had to be accessible somehow.

It was similar to my uncle's doorbell in that it was a doorbell/camera combo like a Ring. Shouldn't it be sending alerts that someone was at their door? My life would be a whole lot easier if they just came to the door instead of having to summon them.

I tried the handle on the security gate; it was locked. I stretched my arm between the bars as far as it could go, then rotated my shoulder, but still couldn't push the button. I scanned the yard until my eyes eventually rested on a stick. I grabbed it, and with a lot of maneuvering, was finally able to ring the doorbell.

"What do you want?" A scratchy, kind of deep voice demanded through the intercom. Was it the lady or the man? It was hard to tell.

"Hi, um," I started. "I live across the street." I thumbed over my shoulder. "We sorta met last night."

"And?" she said, sounding more feminine after clearing her throat.

"I'm really sorry to bother you, but I think Bojangles went into your yard."

"Who's Bojangles?"

I shifted my weight from one foot to the other. "My dog," I said, then added, "well, my Uncle Larry's dog."

There was an uncomfortable silence–at least for me. "You know, Larry? From across the street?" I added as I waited for some sort of acknowledgment. After none, I continued, "I wondered if you could go get my dog."

"Stay away!"

I would, but there was the unfortunate situation with *Larry's* dog being on *her* property. "Or if you could open the gate, I could grab him."

"Don't go near the fence!" she bellowed, then exhaled loudly.

I stepped back. What would she suggest I do that would actually accomplish something? "Okay. Should I just meet you over there?"

"No."

I retreated farther from the front porch and backed into a rose bush. A thorn grabbed my skin. "Ouch!" I looked down to see a spot of blood on my calf and my shoe sinking into the soft dirt of a newly planted bush. In my state of panic, I hadn't noticed the smell of manure. Or possibly it was just stronger over here. It must've been some sort of fertilizer that I had stepped in.

I positioned myself so I could watch the front door and the wooden gate to the left at the same time (and distance myself from the smell) and waited for her to come out. After what seemed like forever, but probably just a few minutes, I threw caution to the wind and approached the side gate. Although I was keenly aware of the "NO TRESPASSING" signs, I could not lose Bojangles! I boldly peeked through several small knot holes in the wood panels, hoping to catch a glimpse of...something. Anything. Not being able

Neighborhood Watch

to see anything, I stood on my tip-toes and looked over the fence. It wasn't enough to give me a clear view, so I stepped on a cement block which was pushed against the base of the fence and looked over.

And looked directly into the lady's eyes.

"Aagh!" I yelled and jumped back.

"I thought I told you not to bother the gate," she said, her tone chastising. She looked different from what I pictured her from seeing her in the dark–older. She was shorter than me with frizzy, gray hair that came to her shoulders. Her face was round and wrinkly, but not in a sweet, grandma way. She wore a stained white shirt and baggy chambray pants with an elastic waist.

"I was trying to be helpful," I said in my defense.

"You're not being helpful. You're being nosey."

I squinted at her, trying to decipher what exactly I was missing. "I'm really sorry I disturbed you, but I'm just trying to get Bojangles back. He ran off when he heard your dogs."

"I don't have dogs," she snapped.

I was pretty sure she *did* have dogs. None of this made sense. "I heard dogs," I insisted.

"Must've been someone else's dogs."

"But it came from your yard," I said.

"How could it? I don't have dogs."

Her hard eyes locked with mine, daring me to argue.

I dropped my eyes. "Do you see my dog?"

"Glen?" She yelled without taking her eyes off me. "Did you find a dog?"

A few seconds later, the man approached. He was tall enough that his bald head was visible above the fence. "Is this the pup you're looking for?" He held Bojangles high in the air reminiscent of the scene with Simba from *The Lion King*.

My breath came out in a whoosh. "Yes! That's him!"

The gate opened with a high-pitched squeak and a loud scraping sound. The gap was just wide enough to fit the man. Up close, he was older than I had pictured. He had a long, white beard and his skin was weather-worn. He looked like a retired biker dude, except that instead of a leather jacket, he wore a plaid, flannel button-down over denim overalls.

I snatched Bojangles. Once the man released the dog, he stepped back, and I caught a glimpse of the yard. I saw a stone structure that looked like it could be the oven my uncle told me about. There were also more freshly planted rose bushes along with the empty black, plastic containers they came in. Like the front yard, the planting looked very haphazard. It was hard for me to imagine Mean and Nasty Crazy Lady was one of those attentive gardeners who talked to her plants and flowers. Or she could be a crazy gardener like in a Stephen King novel. But who knew? Maybe we really did get off on the wrong foot.

Maybe I should buy her a plant as an apology gift.

You know, something invasive.

Like mint.

"Thank you," I said sincerely. I really did appreciate their help rescuing Bojangles from them. I couldn't imagine having to make that phone call to my uncle that I had lost his beloved dog less than twenty-four hours in my care. He might stroke out.

I quickly stepped out of the way as the gate slammed in my face. I scurried back home, clutching Bojangles and his unattached leash.

Once in the safety of Larry's house, I collapsed into the recliner. I panted like a dog on a hot day as I waited for the adrenaline to stop pumping through my body .

"Bojangles," I said, holding the dog so he was looking directly at me. "Do not ever do that again. Those are scary people!"

His eyes met mine and I took that as a sign of agreement.

And then he dropped something on my lap.

It was a bone.

Chapter 5

Now Seemed Like a Good Time to Get the Mail

The bone lived in my head rent-free for hours. Because, like, where'd it come from? Obviously the neighbor's yard, but still. What kind of bone was it? It was small–but did it come from a human finger or leftover KFC? Was it in the ground or in the trash? I used Google Lens trying to identify it. I was pretty sure it was chicken and not human. Or at least that's what I kept telling myself. Then I looked up chicken bones. They looked very similar to what Bojangles had found. It *had* to be a chicken bone. It was definitely a chicken bone. I was so confident it was a chicken bone, I threw it in the trash and told myself I'd forget about it.

Finally, at bedtime, I reclined in the chair in the front room and turned on an episode of *What the Heck?!* hoping to distract my thoughts away from the bone. With as hard as I tried to convince myself it was just an innocent chicken bone, choosing a podcast episode about a guy named Harry who cut up his victims with a hacksaw probably wasn't the best choice.

The first time the chime of the motion sensor woke me,

Neighborhood Watch

followed by Bojangles barking, it scared me. *Hacksaw Harry?* It took me a few seconds to realize where I was and that there wasn't a serial killer at the door, just the motion detection notification going off. By the time I drifted off to sleep, the notification woke me up. Again. And Bojangles barked. Again. What was going on out there? This time, I gave up ignoring it and gave in to curiosity. A quick peek out the window confirmed it was, indeed, the neighbors once again out in the dead of night, unloading stuff from the back of their car. I watched until they were done doing whatever it was they were doing and decided nothing sinister was going on. After that, I drifted back to sleep

* * *

A beeping woke me and sent Bojangles into barking mode. I sat up straight in the chair. *Hacksaw Harry? An alarm? The smoke detector?* I looked around trying to locate where the noise was coming from. Outside? I swept the curtain aside, a little more awake. After being temporarily blinded by the bright sunlight, I focused my eyes. I didn't see a serial killer out there, but the smiley arrow face of the Amazon delivery truck.

Amazon!

I exhaled and started breathing normally.

I had never been so happy to see Amazon in my life! My blue light glasses had arrived! Oh, the possibilities! Social media! TV! Scrolling on my phone! Bojangles was less than enthused that Amazon was here and refused to move from his spot on the end of the chair and continued barking. I swung my leg over him so I could get a better look outside. That way I could properly anticipate the package about to be put on my doorstep.

The truck didn't park in front of Larry's driveway, but did a three-point turn at the end of the cul-de-sac and parked parallel to the Milton's. A guy with dreadlocks jumped out and hustled to the back of the truck. He stacked three medium-sized boxes on a hand truck and carried an envelope, then walked confidently toward their door.

How does he deliver the packages? Especially since they had the gate at the entrance and the hard-to-reach doorbell. *Has he had any run-ins with the neighbors?* They probably wouldn't chase him off the property for delivering packages.

From where I was, it looked like he just set them down in front of the gate. He didn't even *try* to ring the doorbell.

I held my breath as the delivery guy returned to the truck, and emerged again with a small box. The chime of the motion detector alerted me as he quickly jogged up the driveway. I yanked the door open and forced myself to reach for the package instead of snatching it out of his hands.

My glasses had arrived!

I ripped open the box and tried out my new best friends. They were perfect! I settled in the chair and basked in social media. Well, kind of. I scrolled Instagram, seeing all the wedding festivities I was missing out on. It looked fun. More fun than I was having here. The view of the Caribbean beaches was certainly better than my view here. Seeing everyone paired up and the bride and groom looking so happy, made me long for the same thing. And reminded me that I wasn't in a relationship. Or hadn't been for a while now, but suddenly I felt lonely and wished I had someone in my life. I texted Sierra.

Me: How are you feeling?

Again, I didn't expect to hear back immediately, so I continued to scroll Instagram.

Before I had a chance to use up my allotted screen time, my phone display lit up with Larry's number.

"Hi, Larry!" I said.

"How are things?" he asked.

"So far, so good." Because, overall, it had been good. Except for the run-in with the neighbors when I almost lost his precious Bojangles. "Bojangles is a great napping buddy. And we've been going on walks."

"If he's sleeping with you it's a good sign he likes you."

I took that as it was okay for Bojangles to be on the furniture. But I also wasn't going to clarify just in case I was breaking his house rules.

"How's your conference going?"

"About the same as all the other conferences," he said.

Did that mean it was good? Bad? Boring? I had never been to a conference for work, and since I worked in insurance, a conference for that would be boring. But right now, a work conference–whether for insurance or interior design–sounded much more interesting than head rest.

"Hey, my neighbor to the right sent me a link to a neighborhood group page. There was another catalytic converter theft yesterday about two streets over. Keep your eyes peeled."

I thought about what I saw the first night.

Were those neighbors thieves? Would they steal from their own neighbors? Should I be suspicious of them?

If they were thieves, I wouldn't want them stealing Bojangles. I recommitted to figuring out Bojangles's harness.

And I would avoid those neighbors at all cost.

As Larry told me the details, I glanced out the window. And then did a double-take. A police SUV just parked in front of the Milton's.

Oooh! What was going on?

"Larry, there's cops across the street. Can I call you back?"

"Absolutely not! You need to tell me *exactly* what's happening."

"Okay. A male and a female officer just got out of the vehicle and they're walking up to the metal security gate."

"Are their guns drawn?" Larry asked.

"No. But the guy has his hand resting on his gun. I think. It's hard to tell."

"You could go out to the porch. Maybe you can see better from there," he suggested.

I sucked in my breath. "No! Then they'd know I was watching."

"Isla," Larry said, with a hint of chastisement. "Everyone rubbernecks when the cops pull up to the neighbor's house. It's human nature. Isn't that what neighborhood watch is?"

I thought neighborhood watch was neighbors keeping an eye on the neighborhood, not the neighbors. But what did I know? I wasn't a homeowner.

"Isla? What can you see?"

Not much and I didn't have the brazen courage to step outside and openly watch.

"How will they ring the bell?" I wondered out loud. Would they run into the same difficulties I had? I opened my mouth to elaborate and then shut it quickly. I didn't want to confess my "oopsie" to Larry just yet. Stressing him out might mean him stressing me out.

Because curiosity got the best of me, I positioned myself to get a better look without being blatantly obvious by standing in full view. Just then, the female officer looked back. I swear, she looked directly at me.

"Oh, crap!" I said and instinctively stepped back.

"Are they getting arrested?" Larry asked quickly.

"No. I think one of the cops saw me." Had the neighbors reported me to the police?

"It's not a crime to watch what's going on."

His words didn't soothe me. Panic gripped my stomach as I quickly reviewed what had happened in their yard the day before. I hadn't done anything wrong. Maybe trespassed. But it was for a very good reason. I couldn't think of anything else they might be able to accuse me of.

"I'll call you back," I said, too stressed to narrate the situation to Larry while thinking it through in my own head. I ended the call before I heard his response.

Worried, I retreated into the safety of the room. I moved the comfy chair so I could see what was (mostly) going on, but thought (meaning *hoped*) I was out of sight.

Was this really about me, or was there something else going on? Had I witnessed something I shouldn't have the last two nights when they unloaded the car? Perhaps it had to do with the phantom dog that I'd heard when I'd been jarred from my sleep? Or that I'd heard but she denied having? I watched with dread, my gaze glued to the scene unfolding across the street.

After a while, the couple came out of the house, shut the front door, and stood behind the security gate.

Even from my distance, I could see the woman gesticulating. A palm up, as if saying, "Just wait," a curled fist to her chest in concern. It was still hard to see, so I opened my camera lens and zoomed in. I was able to see better, but not good enough to see facial expressions. After a few more palms up, head shakes, nods, the couple disappeared into the recesses of their house.

From my vantage point, they seemed unhappy with their encounter. But then again, who would be happy with a visit from the police unless you were the one who called them? Especially if they were guilty of whatever they were reported for or doing something illegal.

Less than a minute later, before the officers even returned to their truck, the couple was back outside. They exited and locked the security gate, hopped in the car and backed out of the driveway. The police didn't follow them.

What was going on with the strange neighbors? I wanted to ask the police and ask, but also didn't. What if it *was* about me? Even if it *wasn't* about me, they probably couldn't tell me anything, anyway. Wouldn't they have to keep things confidential? Police always say on TV that they can't comment on something that is part of an "ongoing investigation." This probably qualified as an ongoing investigation.

Although...I hadn't gotten the mail since I'd been here.

And now seemed like a good time to get the mail.

That was benign enough.

If they didn't say anything to me, I'd assume the visit wasn't about me.

If they did say something to me...I'd probably throw up on their shoes.

Oh! What the heck? Why not? I didn't have anything better to do. And if they did arrest me, I could just claim my temporary brain injury as the reason behind my behavior.

Did I dare?

My heart thudded in my chest as I considered taking the risk.

I was going to do it!

Never before had getting the mail felt so scary. I grabbed the mail key, slipped into my flip-flops, donned my dark sunglasses, pulled on a baseball cap and with a deep breath, stepped outside.

Neighborhood Watch

Despite my protective gear, the brightness hit me like a punch in the face. I recoiled and immediately adjusted the bill of my cap to angle down sharply.

I was pretty sure I just made myself look *that* much more suspicious.

Would it look even more suspicious if I turned around and stepped back into the house? Was I too far committed at this point to abandon my mission and retreat?

"Isla," I said out loud to myself in a low, but encouraging voice, "they probably won't even notice you."

I paced my steps down the driveway to the edge of the property. The more I tried to relax and act normal, the more convinced I was that I looked guilty.

Of what? Nothing. Okay, maybe being incredibly nosey.

And bored. Let's not forget bored.

But being nosey and bored was *not* a crime.

I released the latch on the black, metal mailbox, noting how quaint it was to have "old-fashioned" mail boxes lining the streets of the neighborhood. Where I lived, it was an ugly, gray community box in a dirty, outside room at my apartment complex.

I was rewarded with several envelopes and the weekly grocery flyers. I flipped through the mail, really playing up the part of attentive mail-getter, but didn't see anything important. It was mostly junk mail that I'd recycle once in the house.

"Excuse me."

The female officer spoke first.

I froze. *Uh oh!*

I turned and the two officers stood about five feet from me. The female officer had dark hair pulled tightly in a bun, olive skin and the name "Morales" embroidered on her vest. The male officer's name was Nettles and he had brown hair cropped close to his head and looked too young to be a cop. And too attractive. Instead, he could've been a model for a "Man in Uniform" calendar with his blue eyes and perfect face. His eyes were probably the closest thing I'd get to seeing the Caribbean Sea.

"Hi? Yes?" I stammered, thrown by his good looks and their presence in general. I didn't seem awkward or suspicious *at all*.

"Do you live here?" She nodded to Larry's house.

"No. Yes. I mean..." I struggled for the appropriate response.

"Yes, you do, or no, you don't?" Morales asked.

I shook my head slowly, careful to be gentle with my brain. "I'm house-sitting for my uncle. He lives here."

"Do you know the neighbors by chance?" Officer Nettles asked and thumbed over his shoulder.

"I've only been here three days."

"Have you seen anything suspicious going on in the neighborhood?" he asked.

I squinted at him. "What would you consider suspicious?" The neighbors' very existence seemed a bit suspicious to me, but that didn't mean it was.

"They think someone is spying on them," Morales said.

My heartbeat quickened and sweat broke out on the back of my neck. "I hope it's not me," I blurted out. "My dog —my uncle's dog—ran into their yard yesterday and I had to ask them to get him. I wasn't spying on them." Had they reported me?

"Do they have a dog as well?"

I shifted my feet. "See, here's the weird thing. I thought I heard a dog when I was trying to get Bojangles."

"Bo who?" Morales asked.

"Bojangles. My uncle's dog."

The officers nodded as if they understood.

"But when I asked the lady about it, she flat out lied. She completely denied having a dog. But I was *sure* I heard one."

"Did you see a dog?" Nettles asked.

I shook my head. "No."

"Did you go into their house or their backyard?" Nettles asked.

"Nope. They seem pretty guarded."

"So, you didn't see anything in the backyard?" Morales confirmed.

Like a kiln to fire ceramics...or burn trespassers? "Nope." The chicken bone in the trash came to mind. Should I dig it out and hand it over? I was sure it was nothing. It had to be nothing. What if it was just an innocent chicken bone and *I* looked like the crazy one?

Morales continued. "Or anything inside?"

"Nope. They were more 'keep out' than 'come on in', if you know what I mean."

"How about the garage?"

I shook my head. What were the officers looking for? Were the neighbors being investigated? Or was I? I really, really hoped I wasn't involved in any way.

"Although...," I said.

"Yes?" Nettles asked.

Our eyes met and my heart stuttered. Was he suspicious of me? Or did he just know how attractive he was?

"They've been outside at one or two in the morning the last couple of days." I might as well throw it out there. Maybe it would help solve whatever case they were working on.

"What were they doing?" Nettles asked.

I leaned in and dropped my voice. I think I caught a

hint of his aftershave. "Not sure. It seemed they were unloading stuff from the car the first night. Last night, I don't know."

Both officers nodded but remained silent.

"It's weird to me," I continued, in full-on babble mode now, "that they're doing stuff when they should be sleeping. I mean, look at them, they're old! It's not like they're just getting home from working the swing shift."

Morales glanced at Nettles before speaking. "Do you know if they work?"

"I really don't know anything about them other than they seem paranoid and weird," I said with a shrug.

"Is there a lot of traffic coming and going?" he asked.

I thought for a second. "They get a lot of deliveries."

"How about visitors? People stopping in for a short amount of time?"

"Are they drug dealers?" I asked, genuinely shocked. They seemed too old to be drug dealers.

Morales shrugged. "Or just running a business."

Like a meth lab? Shows that I had binge-watched years ago popped into my mind. Was I witnessing my own version of *Breaking Bad*? Or could they be laundering money like in *Ozark*?

"Okay," Nettles said. He pulled out a card and handed it to me. "If you see anything suspicious, contact us."

"Like what kind of suspicious?"

"Anything you think is out of the ordinary."

More out of the ordinary than what I'd already told him?

I looked at the card. Nathan Nettles. Code Enforcement.

They were here on a code violation? That was it?

A little voice inside my head said the only one in code violation was Officer Hottie for being so dang attractive.

I distracted myself from my intrusive thoughts by running my finger along the edge of the card. *Is that his personal number on the card?*

"Okay, I will," I said.

"Thank you," Officer Morales said.

"Yes. Thank you," Officer Nettles said. "And what was your name again?"

"Isla. It's Isla Wilson."

"Isla. Remember to call us if you need us," Officer Nettles said before the two of them headed back to their vehicle.

If only he could come back for me and not just because the couple seemed super suspicious.

Chapter 6

Something Was Up With the Neighbors!

Back inside, I watched out the window until the police drove off.

Besides getting the scoop on the neighbor situation, and hoping Officer Nettles would *have* to come back, the only other important thing to do today was make decisions: what to eat...what to do...what to eat....

I reclined in the comfy chair and closed my eyes, knowing I was *supposed* to sleep, but I didn't *want* to sleep. My mind was abuzz with questions. The overstimulation of being outside and the conversation had my tired brain working overtime to process everything that had just happened.

So, something *was* up with the neighbors.

I knew it!

And the police showing up confirmed it.

And Nettles was hot! Was he married? But that was a moot point, so I needed to focus on the situation right in front of me.

What was going on?

Were they running a puppy mill? A dog-fighting ring?

A cock-fighting ring? Hoarding cats? Selling eggs from "free-range" chickens without a permit? Raw goat milk? Sheep milk? Or was it drugs or money laundering?

Had someone else thought they'd seen something suspicious and reported it?

Were they just misunderstood old people?

Could it be a simple code violation?

Or could it be something more nefarious?

Or could it be my concussion?

Or my penchant for listening to true crime podcasts?

I squeezed my eyes tight and tried to shut my thoughts off. I pictured the ocean and concentrated on breathing with the rhythm of the imaginary waves. In. Out. In. Out. My mind wandered to the other night. What were they unloading? What were they up to?

I needed to sleep, but couldn't. So many questions came to mind. So many unanswered questions.

I gave up and sat up. I glanced at my watch. It'd been twenty minutes. I could take my meds, but that always made me feel groggy when I woke up. I contemplated what to do.

The quiet was interrupted when the doorbell chimed. It was followed by a brisk knock on the front door.

Officer Nettles?

Bojangles beat me to the front door, barking like crazy. I scooped him into my arm, trying to quiet him.

I glanced out the side panel window beside the door. It was Mildred! *And* she saw me.

Surprised, I pressed my back flat against the door, and hid behind its safety. My breaths came quickly.

Why was she here?

Pounding vibrated through the door. I had to open it—

there was no way I could pretend I wasn't home—she'd already seen me.

With a couple of deep breaths, I stepped back and opened the door.

Bojangles growled, baring his teeth and mustering all the ferociousness a ten pound dog could. I gripped him tighter, afraid he might slip out of my hold and bite Mildred on the ankle.

I planned to keep a neutral expression, hoping to come off as oblivious to why she'd be here. But I didn't get the chance.

"I know you called the police," she hissed.

Taken aback, I shook my head. "What?"

"You called the police!" She stepped forward with each word until she was practically in my face.

I instinctively stepped back and gripped the doorknob to steady myself. "No, I didn't."

"Where's Larry? I want to talk to Larry right now!"

"He's out of town. You'll have to wait until he gets back to–" I was going to say *complain*, but thought I'd better not. That would probably just provoke her. "You can talk to him when he gets back." Or she could call him, but I wasn't going to suggest it.

She shook her crooked index finger at me. "We didn't have any problems until you arrived."

I was still shocked by her accusation. She thought it was *me?* "Why would I call the police?"

"We're just minding our own business. That's what we're doing!"

"If you're not doing anything wrong, why not just let the police in?"

"You don't know who you're dealing with!" she said.

I was about to ask her who, exactly, I *was* dealing with, but didn't get the chance.

"We're minding our own business and you're making things up about us," she said, spittle flying.

She really *was* crazy.

I readjusted my hold on the knob, just in case I needed to slam the door in her face. "I'm not making anything up. I don't even know you."

"Don't think we don't see you. Snooping. Pretending your dog got loose so you can look around."

Paranoid much? She just confirmed my suspicions.

"I'm not doing anything wrong!"

She wagged her finger at me menacingly. "I'm watching you." She turned on her heel and marched off.

"Well, that's great, because you know what? I'll be watching you too!" I yelled at her back. She didn't react or even respond.

Maybe she hadn't heard me.

But she'd better believe I'd be watching them now!

Even if they weren't doing anything wrong, I'd make them feel like they were.

So, there!

I slammed the door and burst into tears. I had literally done nothing wrong except lose Bojangles. "What's her problem?" I asked Bojangles as I picked him up. "I'm not the bad guy. She's just crazy."

Bojangles licked my cheek to express his support.

After a few minutes, I wiped my tear-streaked cheeks. I wasn't sure why I was so upset other than the excess adrenaline.

But one thing I knew: she was not going to intimidate me. Or...at least I'd try not to let her intimidate me again.

I straightened, trying to shake off the confrontation. My

head pounded. I'd done too much. I'd heard too much. I'd stayed up too long. I definitely needed a headache pill. At least it would make me tired and I could think about nothing for a while.

"Come on, Bojangles," I said once I was settled on the chair. "It's nap time."

Even with a pill in my system, Bojangles by my side, and a sleep mask on my eyes, I wasn't sure I'd be able to sleep.

* * *

I woke up to *that* chime and Bojangles barking. The motion detection notifications from the door cam definitely needed to stop because they had already happened several times a night, always accompanied by Bojangles.

Was it the neighbors? What was out there? I moved the curtains aside–it was still daytime–and there was a FedEx truck across the street at the Milton's. The driver climbed in the truck and took off.

Frustrated with being woken up, yet again, I took matters into my own hands. Instead of asking Larry to adjust the sensitivity to motion through the app, I took the battery pack out of the doorbell. I'd mention it to Larry later. I couldn't take the constant disruption.

Now what? I checked my phone to see if I'd gotten any texts while I was asleep. Sierra finally texted back: she didn't have the flu, she had Covid. I sent my apologies and well-wishes and silently gave thanks that I wasn't around to catch it.

Lola sent a GIF scene from the show *The Office* of Jim rolling his eyes, with the message: typical break room drama.

Neighborhood Watch

I guessed the drama had something to do with food left in the fridge. There were constant emails regarding office policy about the break room. Her communication provided little entertainment for me and I moved onto the next text. My parents had sent a picture of the view of the ocean from their room and a note that they hoped I was relaxing. I sighed and clicked on the next text. It was from Larry.

Larry: I got a message from the water department that they detected a continuous flow of water from inside the house. I'm pretty sure it's the downstairs bathroom toilet. I've had problems with it before. Would you go down and shut the water off for me? Just turn the handle that looks like this and is located behind the toilet.

He included a picture from The Home Depot website that showed the thing I needed to turn.

I set my phone down and looked around. Wasn't this a one-story house? "What downstairs bathroom?" I asked Bojangles. The dog looked at me, but, of course, didn't answer.

It took me a moment to realize where, exactly, the "downstairs" bathroom was. This was not a two-story house, so the only downstairs was the basement.

Anxiety wiggled its way into my stomach. Basements weren't my favorite place to go. In fact, unless it was completely finished, I generally avoided them. Larry had said his basement just needed renovation, not finishing. Maybe it was okay.

As I opened the door that led to Larry's basement, memories of my grandma's unfinished, dimly-lit basement popped in my head along with the time my cousin had lied about bodies being buried down there.

Although Grandma's small, Depression-era house had been cluttered and cramped, it in no way compared to her basement, where old household things went to die and never be dealt with again.

When I helped my family clean out her house, the basement and attic were the worst of the worst when it came to collected stuff. Grandma had all sorts of creepy things like clowns, pitchforks, live spiders in the corners and a huge, scary, metal furnace in her basement. Things that made me not want to ever go down there–not with my parents, not with my siblings, and *definitely* not with my cousins.

I stood at the top of the stairs and flicked the light switch on. Bright lights sprung on to reveal moss-green carpeted stairs. If the carpet was the only scary thing about the basement, I could handle that. With a deep breath, I faced my childhood fears and stepped onto the first step. "Come on, Bojangles," I called out, not wanting to do this task alone. Bojangles sat at the edge of the door, but didn't move.

"Come on, puppy. Don't be nervous," I said, despite being nervous. Obviously, Bojangles was the smart one in this situation, but I had no choice. I was the adult and had to handle the problem.

With each step down the shag-carpeted stairs, I reassured myself. This was my uncle's house and he wouldn't have a creepy basement. The stairs were carpeted, not bare wood. That was already much nicer than grandma's basement had been. It was bright and obviously had more than just a single, bare bulb lighting up the room. It didn't smell damp, dank or dusty. Well, maybe a little dusty, but so did my apartment. Who was I to judge someone for a little dust?

At the bottom of the stairs, I scanned left to right and was pleasantly surprised to see a room that was much better than I had envisioned. Granted, it had wood-paneled walls, but was sparsely furnished with some mismatched love seats and had a bunch of plastic storage bins stacked neatly against a back wall and no eerie shadows.

Tucked neatly under the staircase, I found the half bathroom with the offending toilet. Without overthinking it, I held my breath, reached down and turned the handle that matched the one in the picture Larry had sent. Two seconds later, a very quiet hissing stopped and I took that as mission: completed. I bolted up the stairs and slammed the door.

Good thing Larry was paying me so well for this week. I had just earned it.

Back upstairs in the comfort of the chair and Bojangles in my arms, I caught my breath. I rejoiced in the fact that there should be no more reasons for me to go back in that basement for the rest of my visit.

Chapter 7
What I Saw That Night Was Definitely Suspicious

My late-afternoon nap wasn't restful, despite sleeping three hours. My dreams were filled with Mildred yelling and chasing me, being taken hostage by her in my uncle's basement, and then somehow ending up at that weird outside oven in her backyard. Were the pills making me have these disturbing dreams or was it from what I saw going on across the street? I needed to read the side effects information for the medicine, but I didn't have it with me and would have to look it up online. I certainly didn't want to waste my precious screen time reading up on drug facts. I'd wait on that for now.

I took a lap around the house, ate a handful of granola, then returned to the seat. I closed my eyes and repeated some cognitive shuffling exercises my doctor had given me. Typically used for anxiety or over-thinking when trying to sleep, the exercise was supposed to calm the mind by choosing a word and using the spelling to think of random, unrelated words.

But it wasn't sleep I craved. And it wasn't mind relaxation. It was excitement. I had cabin fever. Eventually, I gave into the boredom and harnessed Bojangles up before the sun had even started setting. Bojangles and I could take our walk early.

The walk helped–a little. A very little. Afterwards, I picked up my phone and dialed my uncle. He'd be able to give me more of a scoop on the neighbors.

Larry answered with a question. "How's Bojangles?"

"He's good. We're good." I still wasn't ready to tell him about the leash escapade. "And I took the batteries out of your doorbell and motion detector. That thing is seriously on a hair trigger."

"Okay. I wondered why I wasn't getting any alerts on the app."

"And I had a run-in with your neighbor across the street."

"Mildred or Glen?"

"Her."

"He's nicer than she is."

"That wouldn't take much effort," I said.

Larry cracked up.

I peeked out the curtain to see if anything more was happening. It looked still. "She was mad about Code Enforcement showing up at their house."

Larry let out a low whistle. "Someone reported them again?"

"Again? She thought it was me and came over and tore me a new one!"

"She's suspicious by nature," Larry said.

"How do you know?" Had he seen that side of her before?

"Look at all the bars on the house. She's a hoarder. She probably thinks all the stuff is valuable and someone's going to break in and steal it. And how many truck loads would *that* take?"

She could be mentally ill or had some sort of trauma. "Seriously, though. What's going on with them?" I asked.

"Whatever it is, it's disgraceful! They're an embarrassment to the neighborhood. The front patio area is completely packed with stuff. Actually, it's gotten better. Like, before, you couldn't even see their front window."

Had Larry reported them the first time?

"Really?" It was so bizarre for me to think you had a window, but you couldn't see out of it.

"It used to have boxes and stuff piled high outside. The whole side yard was full. They put that wooden fence up to hide it. It's only recently that they cleaned up their yard because they were reported to Code Enforcement."

"Interesting," I said, digesting the information as I stared at the house. If Code Enforcement had been called before, why would she think it was me? "Why do you think they were called again?"

"I don't know. Maybe their backyard is filling up. Or that their front porch and garage are a fire hazard. If you happen to see their garage when it's opened, you'll see its jammed packed within an inch of the door. Kindling. Poof!"

An image of a house bursting into flames popped into my head. But I didn't get the feeling it was that. "The police were more interested in finding out if they had a dog or if they had a lot of visitors."

There was a quick intake of breath. "You talked to the cops?"

"Yes," I said. I was slightly embarrassed to admit it.

"Did they, like, knock on the door? Go around the neighborhood asking questions? What is going on? I need all the details."

"I was getting the mail."

"Uh huh. Convenient," Larry said, the sarcasm heavy.

"I told them I heard a dog, but Mildred denied having one."

"I wonder why Animal Control wasn't called instead. Or maybe that department is part of the recent budget cuts."

I perked up. "So, they *do* have a dog?" I asked.

"They used to, but maybe it's passed away. I've had conversations with her about it. She once told me she was worried someone would kidnap her dog."

Unless it had risen from the dead, it was still alive. There *had* been a dog there.

As I sat in the chair, watching their property from my darkened house, an idea came to mind. What if I did something that would soothe Madhouse Mildred? I contemplated how to approach her.

"Should I try to do something about it? Bring them a batch of cookies or a pot of geraniums?" The idea of a mint plant crossed my mind once again.

"She'd probably accuse you of poisoning them. Just stay out of their way. They may be a little crazy, but I think they're harmless. It's easier to just avoid them."

Surely they couldn't always be this grouchy all the time to all the neighbors, right? "But maybe cookies would make her think it wasn't me who reported her."

"You're only there until the end of the week. It'll all blow over and be fine," Larry said.

"Okay," I said. Mentally I committed to staying out of their way. "Have a good night and we'll talk again tomorrow."

"Give Bojangles my love."

"I will," I said and hung up.

Sally Johnson

* * *

That night, I awoke about 2 a.m. It was as if my body had a natural alarm clock and I was now on that weird schedule. Without hesitation, and conveniently being in the chair, I gently pushed the curtain aside with my toe to check if there was any movement with the neighbors. I hated to admit it, but I was hooked.

I was not left disappointed. Mildred and Glen were unloading stuff from the car again. The conversation with the police popped into my head. *Could* they be drug dealers? Was that *really* why the cops had come? I could gather evidence and it would give me an excuse to call Officer Nettles.

I watched, straining to see what they unpacked from the car. With only the moon as my source of light, and a dim, yellow sliver from a streetlight, my line of vision was not well-illuminated. Should I go out there? If I opened a window, they'd probably hear it. Or...I could go out the back door and walk around to the front yard. That would provide a quiet exit and the shadows of the night, a veil of invisibility. Or just low visibility. But that was good enough for me. Would Bojangles bark if I left?

I hoped not, because I was going to do it!

I crept outside into the warm night air, gripping my phone, and tiptoed through the dew-laden grass. There was a tree in Larry's front yard that had a perfect vantage point. After I silently got into position, I realized I should've brought a lawn chair. Standing behind the cover of the tree, I fought the urge to sit. Who knew how long their unloading session would take. The grass was damp with dew, so I didn't want to sit on it, but my legs grew tired easily.

Lounging around all day did nothing for my physical endurance.

Crash!

Metal clattered onto their driveway and the sound reverberated through the quiet night air.

The first crash was followed by a second, smaller crash. It sounded like the clinking of a chain falling.

I held up my phone and started filming. The more I zoomed in, the grainier it got. But still, some evidence was better than no evidence, even if it was bad quality. Or at least that's what I told myself.

"Glen!" Mildred hissed. "You're waking up the neighborhood!"

"Do you want to do it yourself? If not, keep quiet!" Glen shot back in a loud whisper. He bent down to pick up whatever he'd dropped on the driveway.

Mildred didn't move. "You need to keep quiet!"

Glen continued gathering. "You're welcome to help, Mildred."

"You know I can't lift the...They're too heavy for me."

It was hard to decipher everything Mildred said. It sounded like "parts", but could've been "carts." I leaned forward, exposing my hiding place a little, but hoping to hear better.

"You can at least pick these pieces up. You don't want to leave them out for the neighbors to see," Glen said.

What didn't they want us to see? Oh, my gosh! A thought hit me like a bolt of lightning. Were they responsible for the rash of catalytic converter thefts? The metal. The clandestine unloading the back of their car. Could it be possible? Glen was too old, in my opinion, to be on the ground under cars sawing off parts. And Mildred was pretty much useless—I hadn't seen her do anything but boss him around. Maybe they had a gang of thieves that went around with them at night, stealing car parts. Did they own a chop shop? Were they unloading the stolen goods at night?

Glen must've eventually gathered all the evidence up because from where I sat, Mildred didn't help. Once he stopped bending down and standing up, they went inside.

I waited until they set the car alarm before moving. I didn't want to get caught. I didn't need to give her any more reasons to suspect me of anything, even if some of it might be true. Out of habit, I adjusted the curtains so I could look across the street. What secrets did that house hold?

Back inside, I reviewed my footage. It was horrible and useless. You could barely make out anything that was going on. I needed to investigate this further. A pair of binoculars would help. Then I could ~~spy~~ see more effectively, day or night, and be less likely to be caught. Maybe then, with some surveillance, I could figure out what was really going on there.

I wasn't going to look in their windows or anything. I'd just be getting a better view of what was going on outside and in the middle of the night. I figured anything done out in the open was free game for onlookers. I didn't need to know what was going on inside. That was their business.

It was like an unofficial neighborhood watch, right? Neighbors looking out for each other–making sure crime wasn't happening in *their* neighborhood.

I pulled out my phone and ordered a pair of powerful, yet budget-friendly, night vision binoculars off of Amazon.

The best part: they could be delivered tomorrow.

Chapter 8
I Woke Up With a Crazy Idea

I woke up with a crazy idea.

What if I followed the Miltons today?

The thought not only exhilarated me, but energized me. I had something to do today! I would follow the neighbors and find out what they were up to. Could be slightly illegal, but not really. Even though my day was wide open, due to the limitations of my head rest, I only had a small window of time to do said sleuthing. I hoped Mildred and Glen unknowingly cooperated with my questionable plans.

They did not.

I spent most of the day in the chair, by the front window, staring at their driveway. There was no movement–not even a glimpse of them outside. How was I going to follow them if they didn't go anywhere? And they needed to go out in the daytime, because driving at night with all the car headlights was a guaranteed headache for me.

I dozed out of boredom a few times, but every time I woke up, the first thing I did was check their driveway. Their car hadn't moved.

"There's always tomorrow, Bojangles," I said out loud, as if *he* was the one who was disappointed.

Bojangles' ears perked up. Poor guy, I was a boring, neighbor-obsessed, suspicious dog-sitter that was probably reading into a totally benign situation out of desperation for entertainment. He'd been stuck inside all day while I anticipated following the crazy neighbors. Who sounded crazy now?

Giving up, but internally committing to continue my watch later, I stood and stretched. Doing nothing all day was exhausting. I still had to walk Bojangles, and now was as good a time as ever, so I retrieved the leash.

Despite it being peak sunshine, I suited up, put on Bojangles' harness and took him for the long-awaited walk. I would brave the sunshine and do something nice for the dog who had been nothing but patient all day.

I was rewarded for my good deed of walking the dog and getting a little exercise myself. When I turned the corner into the cul-de-sac, I heard voices.

"C'mon," Mildred said. "Hurry up."

It was my lucky day! They were still home! They were outside! And getting in their car!

I scooped Bojangles into my arms and hurried the short distance to my uncle's house. I unharnessed him, grabbed the keys and my purse and headed toward the garage. In my haste, I'd forgotten my "protective gear" and came back out with my bucket hat and sunglasses. Not exactly accessories to help me blend in with my surroundings, but I had no choice.

As the garage door creaked open, announcing to everyone it was opening, I was glad to see the neighbors' car was still in the driveway. I climbed in the BMW, rolled down the windows and adjusted the rearview mirror. I would sit, listen and observe.

The back door of their SUV was ajar, and Glen loaded trash bags into it. Big, black trash bags with heavy, sagging bottoms. The view wasn't great (note to self: check on order for binoculars), but I could tell by the shape of the bags that the contents had to be soft and not formed, like, say, sand and not boxes. It could be a body (or body parts) in there. Were they murderers too?

I continued, vigilant, until the task came to an end. Five trash bags in total had been put in the car. Trash day was tomorrow. "Interesting that they didn't put it into the cans," I said to myself. The trash cans were lined up on the outer wall of the garage facing the neighboring house, along with the recycling bin. With the amount of packages they received, why weren't the bins overflowing with boxes? "Maybe it's just lawn and garden debris from last night and they're taking it to the landfill."

Or they were cleaning up. Were they worried that their phantom dog would be removed from their house if it lived in an unclean and unfit environment? Or, because they were hoarders, elder services had been contacted and they were coming to do a safety and wellness check? Whatever it was, I was totally invested in following this story until the end.

Now how to time the "leaving" without seeming too obvious or that I was following them?

I slowly backed out, stopping once I was clear of the garage to close the door. I glanced in the rearview mirror. Mildred was in the car, but Glen's door was ajar. I crept back, letting the idling speed of the engine move the car. No need to hurry since they hadn't gone anywhere. At the end of the driveway, I had a choice. Wait for them to move, or move myself. I chose to move, not wanting to draw undue attention to myself and hoping to act like I was just going out and about, running errands and things. Certainly *not* following them.

By the time I was out of the driveway, they still hadn't moved, although Glen was now in the car with the driver's door shut. I couldn't just wait there for them to move. Instead, I pulled up alongside the mailbox, got out and grabbed the mail. I pretended to sort through it, when I was, in fact, watching them out of the corner of my eye. My gosh! How long does it take to get in your car and leave? They made it like the opposite of an Olympic event–how long could you stretch out the time it took to actually leave.

I held my phone to my ear, pretending to talk. I could snap a picture, but of what? Them sitting in their car in their driveway? Technically, they weren't doing anything wrong.

When they finally left, I waited until they pulled out of the cul-de-sac before putting the car in gear and inching onto the street. At this rate, the recon mission would take all day. Obviously, I literally had all day, but…I could only be out in the daylight for so long before getting a headache. And I was anxious to know their secrets.

Not being well-versed in the art of following a car in traffic while avoiding detection, I tried to stay several car-lengths behind them, but they drove so slow that cars kept passing them. I didn't want to be directly behind them, but it was hard to not inadvertently end up there. If I were more familiar with the town, I might've been able to make an educated guess where they were going and just drive directly there. But I had no idea.

Finally, a right turn indicator lit up and they turned into a large shopping plaza. It was anchored by Home Depot, but there was also an AutoZone, dollar store, pet store and a Walgreens. Each store had potential for them to shop at. I waited at the far end of the parking lot and watched as they circled around the perimeter.

They made their way to the back alley of the stores. Not wanting to get too close or be too obvious, I parked in a loading zone that was (mostly) out of sight and watched. Glen pulled beside a huge, construction dumpster, got out and threw all his trash bags into the metal bin.

I couldn't decide fast enough if I should move in anticipation of them driving by, or wait and see where they went.

And then there was the matter of the trash. What was in those bags? Should I try to find out? Dumpster diving had never been on my bucket list, but secretly, I was willing if it meant I could find out their secret.

I held my breath and ducked as they drove by before resuming my quest.

To dive or not to dive? That was the question.

I was going to go for it!

I shut off the car and jumped out. I stood on the metal footing and balanced on my tiptoes trying to see in. It was too high. There were metal rungs on the side, so I climbed them.

As I peered over the edge, disappointment greeted me. The bags were at the very bottom of the container, which, by the looks of it, had been emptied recently.

I could follow through, climb in and rip open the bags. But what if I couldn't get out? It was at least six feet high. There wasn't a ladder on the inside and I didn't trust my parkour skills (or lack of) to climb out. I could think of nothing worse than getting stuck in a dumpster with no way out.

I retreated back to the car, defeated. What a waste of

time. Would I be able to find them again or had I lost pursuit because of this diversion? I hoped their yellow car would be easy to spot.

I drove around the corner of the strip mall and scanned the parking lot. Binoculars would've been super helpful right about now.

Not to be deterred, I crept up and down the parking aisle, acting as if I were looking for a space. I struck out at Walgreens and the dollar store. But hit the jackpot at AutoZone.

I parked far enough away from them that I could watch and hopefully not be seen. Glen came out a few minutes later with a plastic bag. I couldn't see what was in it.

As they backed out of the parking spot, I started the car, waiting to see what they did next. They went through the drive-thru at Walgreens. So far it seemed like they were just running errands. Next they went into the pet store. I once again put the car into park, choosing a spot in the far reaches of the lot but with enough sight line to watch. It was decision time.

Should I go into the pet store? It wasn't big like a PetsMart. It looked like a small, locally-owned boutique. Outside, there were flowers planted in barrels, several bowls of water, and even a fake, red fire hydrant for dogs to do their business. Was the store big enough for the three of us, or would they quickly spot me and realize it wasn't a coincidence I was in the same store? I had no reason to be there unless I made up an excuse that I needed something for Bojangles. That would work.

I opened the car door, surprised at how quickly my pulse sped up just at the idea of spying on them while being in the confines of a store. I had barely stepped out when they both exited the store empty-handed. That was so quick! Worried they might somehow see me from across the way, I jumped into the driver's seat, slammed the door and slid down low in the seat. I was pretty sure I had avoided detection.

It was back to tailing them in the car.

When they got far enough away that I worried about losing track of them, I inched out of my spot and followed from afar. Eventually, they made their way around the entire parking lot and ended up back at The Home Depot.

Why did they drive by all the stores before returning back to where they started?

Did they know I was following them?

I parked on the opposite side of the Home Depot lot and waited a few minutes before heading into the store. My plan was to find them inside and observe them unnoticed.

Once inside, I walked quickly by the aisles, glancing up and down each one, looking for the familiar figures.

What should I do once I find them?

I hadn't thought this through. And my brain wasn't working at full capacity. I should've given it more thought before impulsively giving into my hare-brained idea. Should I walk up and acknowledge them? Pass it off as 'what a coincidence meeting you here'? Hang back and observe? Pretend I didn't know them or recognize them?

I had yet to locate them after making a quick sweep of the aisles inside, so I went outside to the garden area. I meandered about the trees, the planters, the succulents, the soil–

Someone stepped in front of me, cutting me off. "Why are you following us?"

I was face to face with Mildred. Glen was off to the left, standing behind her.

Getting caught was not a scenario I'd considered. Or that they might confront me.

"Oh gosh! You're scary!" I blurted out and then my mind went blank. I'd meant to say she *scared me*! "I mean, I'm not," I stammered, stepping back. My mind scrambled for a justifiable excuse. "I'm looking for a mint plant. As a gift...for my uncle."

She pointed a chubby sausage finger past my shoulder. "Plants are over there. You're in the fertilizer section."

I scrambled toward the potted plants and hurried to find a mint one. Just for good measure–to prove my reasons for being at the store at the same time as them was authentic–I went to check out and purchased it.

I glanced back. Their eyes were on me the whole time.

Chapter 9

I Narrowly Escaped With My Life

Once I returned home, I immediately took a pill. I needed recovery time in the form of a nap. The combination of being up too long, outside too long and the unexpected confrontation and mission exposure, made my brain feel foggy and my head hurt. Bojangles and I settled into bed and I turned on a true-crime podcast–this one about the disappearance of a girl on vacation. My mind wandered into all sorts of scenarios where I could be a victim like the girl in the story and I had to shut it off. Eventually my eyes felt the familiar heaviness that came with the meds and I drifted off.

A *ding* woke me.

Bojangles immediately started barking.

My eyes flew open and I sat straight up in bed.

What was that noise?

The doorbell?

It couldn't be the doorbell.

It took me a minute to orient myself. How long had I been asleep? Thanks to the black out curtains, the darkened room made it hard to tell what time it was. I reached for my phone and checked. It wasn't nearly as late as I thought it was.

The ding was a notification from Amazon. My package had arrived.

My binoculars!

I stared at the screen, trying to make sense of what I was looking at in the proof-of-delivery picture.

A box. A frog planter with faded, fake, red Geraniums. A gate!

No! No! No! No!

That wasn't Larry's doorstep! It was the *neighbors'* doorstep!

The Miltons' doorstep!

The package had been delivered to the scary neighbors' house!

The package containing the binoculars ordered to spy on them *was delivered to them*.

Crap!

I rubbed the sleep out of my eyes and worked on regulating my breathing. Then I tried to clear my mind and come up with a plan to get my box.

Only, it wasn't that easy.

I had slept terribly, tossing and turning as I dreamed of Mildred. It was a jumbled nightmare of being chased by her, then hiding behind the rock fireplace in the backyard only to burn my hands on it. When I saw the wood fire inside the bottom of it, I realized it was being prepared to offer burnt sacrifices.

I opened and closed my hands just to be sure they weren't *really* burned.

And now I needed to go over there. More nightmare fuel.

I squared my shoulders. I was an adult. They were

adults. It was simply a case of mistaken address and should be easy to fix. Surely they couldn't be upset with me for taking what was rightfully mine.

I suited up in protective gear to face the sunlight (and my fears) and opened the door, only to immediately close it again. I couldn't just march over there and get my package. What if they had brought it inside without checking the address label? Even worse, what if they opened it?

Worst case scenarios popped into my head—they accuse me of stealing, they call the cops on me, they shoot me. Holy moly! My imagination worked overtime coming up with all sorts of stuff. I guess I hadn't been using it enough for day-to-day things and now it was in overdrive.

But I wanted what was mine and wasn't sure if they'd do the right thing and bring it to me. For all I knew, they really were thieves and looked at a mistaken delivery as a windfall.

First, I needed to know what I was up against. I checked through the side window of the front door and was able to get a good view of their yard. Yay! The car wasn't in the driveway. I could literally run over there, hopefully snatch my package, and run back in all of a few minutes and be perfectly fine.

It's fine. It's mine. I'm good. It's fine. It's mine. I'm good.

I chanted the mantra over and over, with each hurried step, as I left the safety of Larry's driveway and walked across the street.

When I stepped over the imagined property line from the street to their yard, my stomach tightened as my anxiety ratcheted up a notch. I looked over my shoulder and scanned the yard for any hint of Mildred and Glen being home.

I glanced up, checking for security cameras. They were

old and, if anything like my grandma had been, were technology-challenged. I knew about the one on the doorbell and figured that was as tech-savvy as they got.

Only, they did have some! I hadn't noticed before! How had I missed them?

There was one under each of the eaves by the front door. I swiveled my head around and located more along the roofline. Horror washed over me as I realized they could be watching me remotely right now! Did they get real-time notifications from their security system? Would a response team show up to check out the property?

But I was only getting what was rightfully mine.

The path I chose gave a wide berth between me and the front door and walkway. I ducked, praying I would go undetected. I hoped I could get eyes on the package instead of just approaching the door. Basically, I wanted my presence to go undetected.

I stood beside the bush at the edge of the walkway and the exterior of the house. I couldn't see the ground from where I was. Dropping down to my hands and knees (a regular occurrence here), I crawled on the concrete, staying close to the bushes. I assumed the shrubbery would hide me and that I could reach out, snatch the package and retreat.

My snatch-and-go plan was great in concept but faulty in reality. My arm was too short. Perhaps I could stick my leg out, hook it with my foot, drag it back in the crook of my ankle and hightail it out of there. That plan seemed more viable since my leg was longer. But not long enough.

Still crawling, I backed out and crouched at the edge of the walkway to collect my thoughts. Maybe I could find something around that I could use to drag the package within reach.

They liked to garden. Shouldn't there be a rake, or a

shovel or a hoe around somewhere? I swiveled my head hoping to locate a tool. Or a weapon.

"Oh, for goodness' sake," I said out loud, fed up with the situation. "It's your package, you big baby, go get it."

I stood, dusted the dirt off my palms and knees, and marched my shaky legs over to the gate and snatched my package up. It was very clearly mine–my name was on the label. The box sported a man using binoculars and just had a shipping label slapped on it. Could the company *be* any *less* discreet?

Proof enough. Satisfied, I–

A noise behind me caught my attention.

It sounded almost like...rubber slowly squeaking. It took my brain a second to process the noise because it sounded familiar. It sounded like...wheels turning into the driveway.

I whipped my head around.

They were home!

Like a deer caught in the headlights, I froze.

I glanced right and then left, but remained planted. My decision-making ability lagged as I worked on an escape route. Or plan. Or anything.

Errrt! The car abruptly stopped and Mildred bolted out of the car. "Hey!" she yelled.

My fight or flight response kicked in and I ran! With my package tucked under my arm like a football, I veered onto their lawn, past the car and toward the street. It was a straight shot to my uncle's house. I could do this! I could make it!

"Stop!" Mildred commanded.

No way! I wasn't about to stop and nothing could make me.

Except for maybe the sound of tires screeching.

A quick check over my shoulder confirmed my fears.

Glen was backing up the car!

The white lights approached faster than I could escape and I stumbled on the loose gravel.

Oof!

My hands shot out to break the fall and the box skidded into the middle of the street.

I hit the ground, scraping my palms and landing on my knee. I looked down at the asphalt, thrilled. I had made it to the street! Off their property. Onto public property. I was safe!

The car halted at the end of their driveway and a door flew open.

Blood pulsed loudly in my ears. Everything else around me was a high-pitched white noise.

They were still coming after me!

I stumbled forward, attempting to pop up and keep running, but was unable to coordinate my head, my feet and my body.

Mildred hurried toward me, her breaths coming out in raspy huffs. "What are you doing in our yard you little thief? What did you steal?" Mildred's ferocity could make a grown man cry. Her voice was scary, like Ursula from *The Little Mermaid* when her true self was revealed.

Finding my feet, I scooped up the package and hurried to cross the invisible line that would put me on my uncle's property.

"Give that to me!" Mildred called out.

I glanced back. She was still in pursuit, shaking a fist in the air. Property line or no property line, she wasn't stopping.

"My order got delivered to your house," I called over my shoulder without slowing down. I wasn't going to give her the opportunity to get close to me.

"Prove it! Let me see!"

I couldn't very well stop and let her examine the box that very clearly displayed it was from a binocular company. Label or no label, the box was a dead giveaway of its contents.

The porch was a few steps away. I could make it. With a leap and a final push, I touched home base. I rushed inside and slammed the door shut in one fluid motion.

Bojangles was barking like crazy.

After clicking the lock, I sunk to the floor, my back against the door as if that could barricade it. My breaths were ragged, my body exhausted. That was the most exertion I'd had in a while–both mentally and physically.

Bojangles continued his vocal security alert and I picked him up in an effort to calm him down–and myself, for that matter. He licked my cheek as I spoke to him. "It's okay, boy," I said in a soothing voice. "It's okay. It's over. We're safe–"

Bang!

"Come out here!"

Bang! Bang! Bang!

Mildred was on the other side of the door!

Bojangles responded with a barrage of barks and a few growls thrown in for good measure.

"I'm not opening the door," I called out. Where was my phone? I felt for it in my pocket. I needed to call 911!

"Give me back my package!" Mildred yelled.

Bojangles continued to provide barking protection. I cradled him in my arms, hoping to soothe him. "It was mine!" I said loudly. "I didn't steal it! It was delivered to the wrong house."

"Prove it!"

Again, I could simply open the door and show her the

box. But...I just couldn't do it because of the contents of the box.

My heart raced and my head pounded. "I don't have to prove anything to you. It's mine. Now leave me alone!"

Bang! Bang! Bang!

Enough! "If you don't leave right now, I'm calling the police!" I yelled with all the authority I could muster.

"You're going to call the police? I'm going to call the police! Now stop messing with us!" Footsteps retreated and I dared to peek out the window beside the door. Mildred was, indeed, walking back to her house.

I exhaled loudly.

I had narrowly escaped with my life...and my binoculars.

Chapter 10

Who Opened This? A Raccoon?

A mandatory excitement-induced rest was in order. But before I could even *think* about resting, I had to check out my new binoculars. Without bothering to find a pair of scissors, I ripped off the packing tape and tore apart the box flaps. Inside was another box securing the binoculars.

Once opened, I pulled them out and ran my hand across the smooth finish. I gave them a quick once over to make sure nothing was damaged before trying them. With a quick zoom in and zoom out, I determined they worked just fine.

I broke them in with a look across the street (of course!). I pulled the strap over my neck, adjusted the eye pieces, focused the lens and watched as the neighbors' house came into enhanced view. The details were sharp–not bad for a budget-friendly pair of binoculars. I panned across the property, looking at things that had been formerly unidentified objects. There were flower pots, empty or half empty bags of soil and fertilizer, coiled hoses, a folded-up treadmill, a radiator, an old tire that had been overtaken by weeds, some boards, dead leaves, containers of antifreeze, windshield washer fluid, and motor oil. It was a whole array of stuff that probably could all be chucked in the trash.

I focused in on their trash cans, noting that, just as suspected, they weren't overflowing. The lids were on with nothing peeking out. And there was nothing–specifically boxes–piled outside the cans.

I panned back to the left side of their house, where the rows of bushes and roses lined the wooden fence. I could see the details of the bushes, the knots in the wood. I brought the front door back into view and could clearly see–

I dropped the binoculars.

They hit my chest with a *THUD*.

A police car stopped in front of the house.

The police were there? Again?

Did it have anything to do with me? And the "stolen package"? I yanked the binoculars off and set them back in the box. In a moment of sheer panic, I grabbed the shipping box and dropped it in the recycle bin just inside the garage entrance.

Chances were they wouldn't even come over to talk to me–

Knock! Knock! Knock!

Uh oh!

Crap! It had to be the police! Mildred had banged on the door last time. And when I peeked out the side window, she saw me. The police would also see me.

Knock! Knock! Knock!

I chanced a look through the window and my fears were confirmed. With a gulp and a deep breath, I opened the door.

"Yes?" My voice sounded wobbly.

Officers Morales and Nettles stood on the porch.

"We got a call from your neighbor saying that you stole their package," Officer Morales said.

Of course Mildred called the police.

I shook my head. "I didn't. It was mine. It was delivered to the wrong house. Like I told you the other day, I'm here visiting my uncle and I don't think Amazon knew where to drop it."

"Did you explain that to them?" Officer Nettles asked.

Man, he was good looking! I wished I wasn't so nervous so I could appreciate him.

I swallowed hard. "I didn't get a chance to. Actually, I called it out when they were chasing me down their driveway."

"So you went onto their property to retrieve a package that was mis-delivered?" Officer Morales asked.

"Basically, yes."

"Instead of running, perhaps you could have had a conversation with them," she said.

Which probably would've been the smart thing to do. "You've talked to them. They're weird. And we've had some run-ins."

"What kind of run-ins?"

I took a deep breath and an unsettling feeling overcame me. Was I going to look like the crazy one here? "I told you how my dog got off leash and ran into their yard. Then after you guys left the other day, she stormed over here and accused me of reporting them to you guys.

"Did you?"

"No."

"They also think you are following and harassing them," Officer Morales said.

"I ran into them at Home Depot. She accused me of following them."

"Were you?" Officer Nettles asked.

Yes. "I was buying a mint plant."

"Do you have that mint plant?" he asked.

I pointed to the corner of the porch by his feet. "I have a receipt if you need."

"No need," Officer Nettles said. He continued, "They think someone is watching them."

Beads of sweat broke out along my hairline. I shrugged.

"Have you noticed anything strange going on in the neighborhood?" Officer Morales asked.

"Other than what they're doing?"

"What are they doing?" she asked.

I started the litany of infractions.

"Last night they were digging in the yard and this morning there's a bunch of new rose bushes. I know that might be nothing, but who gardens at two in the morning?"

Officer Morales' looked over her shoulder at their lawn. "They're adding more rose bushes?"

She was obviously addressing the mess of bushes lining the walkway leading up to the gate.

"Right? They don't even take care of the ones they have," I said. "Maybe she's like a plant hoarder, or something."

"Or something," Officer Nettles murmured.

"And it smelled really bad when I went up there."

"She said it was fertilizer. For her rose bushes," Officer Morales said.

"It smelled like horse manure to me," I said. "Like straight horse manure. Could they have a horse in their backyard?"

Officer Morales frowned. "This neighborhood isn't zoned for farm animals. Have you heard a horse?"

"No," I said. "But I'm not outside all the time." Although,

I watched all the time. Well, not *all* the time—just sometimes. "They have to be getting a fresh supply somewhere." Were they hiding a horse and that was why Code Enforcement showed up?

Wouldn't that be weird if they *were* illegally hiding a horse in their backyard? They kept to themselves, but that didn't mean they were doing something illegal. They certainly didn't want me sniffing around, pun intended. And I didn't want to be sniffing around, because, you know, horse manure.

I had more "evidence" to add. "They loaded up trash bags into their car and threw it away in a dumpster. They get a lot of deliveries. They seem to be up every night in the middle of the night."

Officer Nettles furrowed his brow. "And you know that how?"

"I'm recovering from an injury and I'm frequently up at night. They get home and it wakes me up."

"Okay," Officer Morales said. "Could we see the package that you took? Just to confirm it really belonged to you?"

I stepped back from the doorway. "I put it in the recycle bin. Do you want me to grab it out of there?"

She nodded. "Yes."

I told them I would meet them at the front of the garage. I opened the garage door and walked to the recycle bin. I lifted the lid and pointed to the box. "That's it."

"Can you retrieve it for us?" Officer Nettles said.

I couldn't reach it–it was at the bottom of a pretty empty bin. The only other things in there were the box from my blue lens glasses and an empty wine bottle. Even though my uncle had drunk the wine, I felt like it reflected poorly on my credibility.

Neither cop made a move to help me get the package. I ended up tipping the bin on its side and almost crawling in to be able to reach the box. I backed out of the bin, the box firmly grasped in my fingers.

I brushed myself off and handed it over to Officer Nettles.

"Did a raccoon open this?" he asked, taking in the condition of the box.

Heat rushed to my cheeks. It was a bit shredded on the top. "I did."

"Binoculars?" he asked.

I swallowed hard. "Yeah. For...bird watching."

He looked at me, his eyebrow arched. "Are you a big bird watcher?"

"Just since I've been here. There's lots of...activity going on."

He held my gaze for a moment longer than I could maintain his.

I almost asked if that was illegal, but didn't want the answer. Some people might find what I was doing questionable. I didn't think I was crossing the line of invading their privacy if I only watched what was going on outside. I had no intention of crossing that line.

Officer Nettles held up the box. "We're going to show the box to the neighbors, just so they can see for themselves."

Oh, no! Then they'd know! But I couldn't argue with the police. They were *The Police*.

I watched in dread as the officers went across the street to prove to the Miltons the package was really mine.

* * *

After the binocular incident, and when night time finally came, I sent Bojangles outside for a potty break before taking another headache pill. I had taken way too many of those in the last few days. More than I wanted. But I'd also had way more excitement than I ever could've anticipated. I recommitted myself to resting more as I swallowed down the pill.

Images of me stumbling through Mildred's yard–which was an overgrown jungle of brambles and bushes and Marijuana plants–all the while searching for Bojangles, filled my dreams. Panic gripped me as I fruitlessly tried to find the dog and escape her yard.

It was at the point in my dream that a claw-like hand with long, yellowed nails grabbed my ankle that I woke up. I was drenched in sweat and panting. I sat up and rubbed my face with my hands. Looking around the room, I tried to ground myself, but felt completely disoriented in Larry's pitch-black room.

I checked my phone for the time. 3:21 a.m. I needed to keep sleeping.

Shoosh.

But...what was that noise?

Shoosh.

Nope. I was going to ignore it. I wasn't going to look, I wasn't going to get involved. I clasped my hands together over my waist and closed my eyes. I was going back to sleep. I probably looked like a corpse in a coffin. Immediately, I dropped my hands. Maybe a podcast would help–something other than true crime. Those seemed to be adding fear to my dreams and I needed to sleep.

The *shooshing* sound happened again.

I squeezed my eyes shut and tried a cognitive shuffling exercise.

R-E-S-T.
R: Red, Ron, rain, run.
Shoosh.
E: Eat, ear, enter, escape.
Shoosh.
S: Stop, spying, stay, safe.

T: Try, to...this wasn't working. My thoughts kept returning to that noise. What was that noise?

Shoosh.

Try as I might, I couldn't go back to sleep.

Feeling weirdly claustrophobic because of the darkness, I grabbed my phone and headed to the front room. I needed a little natural moonlight and a distraction to shake the feeling that something was wrong.

Bojangles followed me out of the room, so we went out for a quick potty break before settling onto the chair.

Determined to not check up on the neighbors, I forced myself out of my routine of moving aside the curtain. I didn't need any more fuel for my nightmares. I would find a podcast to listen to–something short and inspirational.

That "shooshing" noise continued to repeat at timed intervals before I caved. Might as well give up and give in.

I slowly and carefully moved the curtain–a fraction of an inch at a time–until I had a better view. I didn't want them to have any clue that I was over here spying on them. And now I had binoculars.

I lifted them to my eyes and adjusted the focus.

Bojangles, my trusty co-spy joined me. "What are they doing?" I asked him.

He licked my chin, then settled down across my lap.

Because of the lighting, I couldn't see all the details, but once my eyes adjusted, and I had the binoculars focused properly, I could make out some of the scene. They were in

Neighborhood Watch

their front yard, in front of their patio, gardening—or more precisely, digging–with a shovel. The noise was them digging. The glint of the shovel bounced off the moonlight. Lots of dark blobs were randomly placed around the lawn. Were those plants? More rose bushes? Maybe those lumps were bags of soil. I watched for almost an hour as they worked away in the wee hours in the morning.

Did they adhere to some weird theory of gardening? Like it's less stressful for the plant to be planted at night? That was the best reason I could come up with. Or they didn't want anyone to either see what they were doing or know what they were doing. Or they were burying dead bodies?

Maybe this was worth reporting to Officer Nettles.

Chapter 11

Someone Was In the House

When I awoke, I was still in the chair. Today I wasn't so stiff—my body must've adjusted to the new sleeping arrangements.

My attention was immediately drawn to the house across the street. There was movement! "They're up?" I exclaimed out loud, startling Bojangles. He jumped down, stretched, then walked off to do his morning business. I hurried to unblock the doggie door and then immediately returned to my post. At least I didn't have to walk him right away. It was important to be grateful for the little things.

I angled the chair to get a better view and watch what was happening. But it wasn't anything too exciting or suspicious. The Miltons got in their car and left–without packing up garbage bags or unloading boxes.

Fresh rose bushes dotted the lawn, further proving maybe they were just midnight gardeners. I talked myself out of calling Officer Nettles. I didn't want to look foolish.

For now, I was left deciding what else to do other than stare out the window until they returned.

Like...what?

Like...did I want to use up my screen time now? Or save it? Should I spend it scrolling my phone or watch some TV?

I considered checking out the little lemonade hut I'd noticed when Larry picked me up the other night. It was only one or two intersections away. At least, that's how I remembered it.

Feeling the stirrings of cabin fever, I decided to break the rules of my head rest once again and get out of the house for a while. The bright sun was not ideal walking conditions for me, but I needed to have a change in scenery. I grabbed my hat and sunglasses, harnessed up Bojangles and off we went.

The lemonade place was farther than I realized and unreasonably expensive. Just because they threw around words like "organic" and "naturally vegan" didn't justify having to sell a kidney to buy a medium frozen lemonade.

As I slurped the ice-cold treat, careful to take small sips to avoid brain-freeze, I stewed over the money I had wasted. I tried to justify the experience as "priceless" to ease my buyer's remorse, but finally had to settle on just getting out of the house was worth it. (Even though it wasn't.)

As we turned the corner and Larry's house came into sight, I noticed something was different. There was a car in the driveway.

Undercover cops?

I doubted it. I mean, unless they drove faded Honda Civics, which I knew they didn't. But who else could it be?

I approached carefully, observing the surroundings. There wasn't anybody in the car. The front door wasn't forced open. The garage door was down. I didn't see any broken windows.

I unlocked the door and stood at the threshold. "Hello?" I called out, but got no response.

But I could *hear* someone.

Someone was in the house.

Movements. Swishing. Footsteps.

Bojangles growled and pulled at the leash.

Should I let him off the leash so he could attack the intruder? Or would that just alert the intruder that we were back? Should I call the cops? With my luck, Officers Morales and Nettles would respond and declare I was crazy.

I took two more steps and cleared the door. Holding my breath, I looked around.

And then I saw something behind the door.

A vacuum cleaner.

Suddenly, I felt stupid. I exhaled, shut the front door and rested against it.

Oh, yeah, it was Thursday. The cleaning lady was scheduled today.

Too many true-crime podcasts and watching the neighbors out the front window left my suspicions in overdrive.

Since I didn't have a cleaning lady, I didn't know what I was supposed to do while she was there. Should I stay? Should I leave? Pretend she wasn't in the room when she was in the room and just go about my day? Which basically consisted of laying around all day and watching the neighbors.

Once unharnessed, Bojangles decided for me, skittering across the room and down the hall, growling, as he sought out the source of the noise. I followed him, hoping to catch him before he attacked the cleaning lady.

He was fast! Faster than me. He disappeared into the

master bedroom and I followed. I stopped short when I found him jumping up at a girl who looked about my age. She was bent over, petting Bojangles.

"Hi, excuse me?" I said as I approached.

She looked up and took out an ear bud. "Hi. Are you Larry's niece?"

"Yeah. I'm Isla."

She walked over and stuck out her hand. "I'm Annie. Nice to meet you." She looked about my age, thin, with short black hair in a pixie cut and a friendly smile.

"Bojangles likes you," I said, noting the obvious affection the dog had for her.

"He's so cute," she said.

Not knowing what else to say, or if I had to say anything at all, I said, "Well, I'll just leave you to whatever you're doing."

"Yeah. Don't mind me. I hope I don't disturb you– usually it's just me and Bojangles and he follows me everywhere."

"Don't worry, I won't follow you everywhere," I said with a small laugh. "I'll be in the living room."

It felt weird trying to sleep while someone worked around me, so I settled into my favorite chair and used the time to scroll through social media, catching up on posts and feeding my FOMO. I scrolled through washing, wiping and vacuuming. I only realized my time was up when the notification appeared on my screen.

What should I do now?

I glanced up just in time to see the Miltons pull into their driveway. There was always the chance that their arrival would provide some sort of entertainment or add a new facet to the mystery I called The Miltons.

I was not left disappointed. Glen unloaded plastic bags–probably groceries–while Mildred waited for him at the front of the car. That, in and of itself, would've been boring, but Glen returned and unloaded some large white bags and a couple of full, black trash bags. Did they load up their trash today but not stop at the dumpster? Weird.

I reached for the binoculars, but remembered Annie was still in the house. I didn't want anyone to witness my dirty little secret. I was hooked. And ashamed to admit it.

Instead, I scooted the chair a little closer to the window.

Last, but not least, Glen carried a new fan and a new drill inside–or that's what the boxes advertised they were.

As footsteps approached from down the hall, I put down my binoculars and grabbed my phone and pretended to be busy. Annie appeared, carrying a small white trash bag which she placed by the door leading to the garage.

I felt the need to make small talk. "Have you worked for Larry long?" I asked.

"For about a year. My mom used to clean for him, but she had knee surgery. I took over some of her clients as a side hustle to pay tuition. I clean several houses in the neighborhood."

My curiosity piqued. "In the immediate neighborhood?" Did she clean for the Miltons? Had someone else actually been inside their house?

She shook her head. "The one next door on this side of the street and the one across the street–"

I pointed to the Milton's house. "There?"

"No. Next to them. My mom approached them once or twice offering her services, but they always said they weren't interested. I've talked to them a couple times and they were totally rude. If anyone in this neighborhood needs their house cleaned, it's probably them."

"And landscapers," I added without thinking.

"Yeah. They have bad taste in landscaping," she agreed.

"And they're always up in the middle of the night planting more rose bushes in their yard."

Her eyebrows went up. "I knew they were weird, but that's crazy. Why?"

I shrugged. "I don't know."

She tilted her head and looked thoughtful. "I've seen them loading their trash bags into their SUV. I mean, trash day is every Friday, why not just throw it out then?"

Excited, I pointed my finger at Annie. "Yes! Me too! It's obviously not a one-time thing."

"Maybe their trash is already full. But I've only seen the two of them."

"Let's look," I said and pointed to the binoculars. Annie seemed like a fellow Milton conspirator, she could probably appreciate my observation methods.

"You've been watching them?" she asked, sounding shocked.

Perhaps I'd misjudged her.

"Well, yes...the cops have been there this week and they're always up in the middle of the night loading or unloading their car. It's suspicious."

"Totally suspicious." She nodded toward the binoculars and took a step closer to where I sat. "What do you see?"

I picked them up and looked at the now-familiar scene. As I focused on the trash, I didn't see anything different or even noteworthy. The lid on the big, blue bin was shut just like it should be.

"Their trash can lid is down and I don't see anything suspicious," I said.

"Dang!"

I panned across the front of the house and my breath

caught. I let go of the binoculars and they hit hard against my chest.

"What? What is it?" Annie asked, reacting to my reaction.

Mildred was outside her front gate, looking at me through her own pair of binoculars!

I yanked them off and dropped them on my lap.

My heart raced and a feeling of dread spread through my body. "Mildred caught me looking at her."

"How do you know?" Annie asked, the surprise obvious in her voice.

"She had binoculars too," I said slowly, trying to process the possible ramifications of the situation. Was I going to get another visit from Mildred? Or maybe another visit from the cops? If so, I could only hope it'd be Officers Morales and Nettles. Or just Nettles.

And at least Annie was here to witness if I had another confrontation with Mildred.

Her eyes widened. "She did? She knows you've been watching her?"

Annie sat on the edge of the stiff couch as I gave a condensed version of my run-ins with Mildred and Glen and included the reasons why I bought the binoculars in the first place. I really hoped Annie would come from a place of no judgment, because suddenly I was questioning my life choices.

"That's completely suspicious behavior," Annie said. "Did you report them to the police?"

"I told them about it when I talked to them."

"I reported them to Code Enforcement for their yard. I've seen rats in their yard when I take the trash out at the neighbor's. It's so gross and a health hazard and my mom told me to report them. They did clean it up, so that's good."

"Did you report them recently?" I asked.

"Yeah. One day their yard smelled so bad I thought something must've died back there. Knowing their history with hoarding crap in the backyard, I filed another complaint."

She had filed the complaints.

Interesting.

It wasn't just me who had concerns.

She looked vaguely in the direction of the Miltons. "I'm cleaning across the street tomorrow and really hope whatever smelled is gone. It smelled like death."

I didn't know what death smelled like, exactly, and hoped I'd never find out. "I think it's the fertilizer they use on the plants."

"Or all the 'plants' they're growing," she said and made air quotes.

"You think they're growing drugs?"

"I don't know," she said with a shrug. "I've smelled someone smoking weed a couple of times. But what I smelled didn't smell like weed or fertilizer. It was disgusting. Like pee. But also bad food. It's hard to describe."

"Huh." What could it be?

She glanced at her watch and then the bag by the door. "I've got to take out the trash."

Starved for human interaction, I really didn't want her to leave. "Do you want to stay for lunch? I've been talking to myself for the last four days and I'm going a little stir crazy. We could order some pizza or something."

She shook her head. "Sorry, I can't. I've got to get to my next client."

"Oh," I said. I didn't do a good job hiding my disappointment and I think she picked up on it.

"Maybe when I'm done tomorrow, we could have

lunch. I'm usually done around one. Then you can tell me if you've seen anything else that's crazy."

My mood immediately lightened. "That'd be awesome. I'll keep my eyes open."

We exchanged numbers and said goodbye.

Chapter 12
Research

After Annie left, I took a nap and then called my uncle. "Mildred and Glen were planting rose bushes in their front yard last night after midnight. There's so much fertilizer over there it smells like a horse pooped all over their lawn."

"How long does horse manure smell?" Larry muttered. I could hear him typing. "It says here about thirty-six hours. I might just narrowly be escaping the stench."

I thought about the police questions and Annie's comment came to mind. "Do you think they're drug dealers?" Like Walter White from *Breaking Bad*? Secretly they have a drug empire that they're running from inside their house?

"I guess they could be. That would explain the fertilizer."

Larry didn't sound overly concerned or surprised by my suggestion. If it were me and my neighbors were as shady as the Miltons, I'd want to know what was up. "But isn't it legal to grow weed here?" So many states had legalized it, I couldn't remember where it was okay.

"Yes and no. Meaning, you have to get a license to grow it," he said.

"Would they grow it in their yard?" That would make sense why they were so worried about me looking over the fence.

"I doubt it. My guess is the basement or possibly some sort of underground greenhouse, bunker or grow building."

Possible explanations popped into my head. "Is their basement a grow house?"

"I'm not home during the day so I don't really know what goes on while I'm at work. But if they were drug dealers, wouldn't there be signs? Nicer cars? Better...fashion?"

I had been home *all* day, and my observations of them left me confused.

My uncle continued. "I really think they're just hoarders and don't want Code Enforcement to come into their house and make them clean up."

"Would they make her clean up her front yard too?"

Larry exhaled loudly. "What she's doing in the front yard with all those plants is a disaster. A complete *eyesore*. Unfortunately, there's no law against bad landscaping," my uncle said with a sigh. "But more importantly, how is my Bojangles?"

I pulled the dog close and got up into his face. "He's being the best boy ever. He's the perfect cuddle buddy." My kind words were rewarded with a lick on the lips. I quickly wiped it off with the back of my hand. I'd seen where his tongue had been recently and I wanted none of that to be on my mouth.

"I miss him. Can you put him on the phone?"

As my uncle spoke in a cutesy voice to his beloved pet, Bojangles licked my phone screen. Gross. I'd have to clean that up after.

"Give him a kiss for me," Larry said.

I considered the prior kiss as kiss enough.

I agreed to check in the next day before I hung up.

I set my phone down and looked at the dog. "Well, Bojangles, what should we do tonight after dinner? Should we nap? Lounge on the chair? Lay on the bed? So many options to do nothing."

Bojangles looked at me and managed to lick me on the lips again before I could turn my face.

I was back to the silence. I could use up the rest of my screen time. I could listen to a podcast, but didn't need more fuel for my over-active imagination. I already had way too many possibilities of criminal behavior in my life.

It must be my imagination...

No! There was definitely something going on over there.

Which led my thoughts back to the Miltons.

I went with screen time, pulled on my blue lens glasses and attempted some armchair sleuthing. First up, property records to confirm I had their correct names. Then I did an internet search of their names, but wasn't able to find out much without entering my credit card info. Neither one of them were on social media (at least that I could find). I shifted the focus of my research on their suspicious behaviors.

Annie also suspected something weird was going on. My uncle thought it might involve drugs. I scoured threads on Reddit, Facebook, Nextdoor and Quora which confirmed my suspicions: some of their behavior fit the behavior of drug dealers. I dug deeper.

I looked up "Maybe it's a Meth House" page on a local government website. It provided common, tell-tale signs of houses or structures being used to produce meth. I went through the checklist.

Outside

- Strong ammonia smell–like strong cat urine. (Maybe. The porch had an odor)
- Covered windows. (Yup.)
- Unusual ventilation to vent the fumes. Opened windows in the winter. (Maybe? It was summer and I couldn't tell.)
- Security systems. (Did bars on the windows, cameras and a Ring doorbell count?)
- Dead spots on their grass from dumping toxic chemical byproducts. (I hadn't seen the whole yard, so, not sure.)
- Excessive trash or unusual trash such as coffee filters, cold medicine packaging, antifreeze, ammonia, paint thinner, starter fluid, camping fuel tanks, batteries, hydrogen peroxide. (I didn't know. I hadn't checked their trash. Should I? But they had cameras and might see me. Or I would accidentally knock over a can and have to pick up disgusting trash. That gave me the ICK.)
- Gloves, masks, duct tape, plastic containers with holes in it. (Not that I'd seen.)

Inside

- A noticeable chemical smell. Area of the house sectioned off or an outside shed or garage. (Didn't know. I hadn't been inside. But they were hoarders, so I sided with messy.)

- Funnels, turkey basters, unusual trash. (I didn't know about funnels or turkey basters, but they sure did have a lot of deliveries which should have resulted in overflowing recycling bins, but I didn't see any evidence of that. There wasn't an abundance of boxes piling up.)
- Strange "equipment" like plastic bottles or fuel tanks with hoses going in or coming out of them. (No idea.)

Behavior of Occupants

- Paranoid. Monitor traffic, suspicious of neighbors, have security systems on their property and around their house. (Okay, this was them! She seemed paranoid and secretive. I didn't know if they monitored traffic. And I was still unsure *how* elaborate their security system was.)
- Stay inside. (Yes, this was them!)
- Smoke outside since volatile chemicals could cause an explosion. (Didn't know if they were smokers.)
- Frequent visitors: dropping things off, picking things up, lots of traffic. (Did delivery guys count? Because they got deliveries. All. The. Time!)
- Burn trash. Store trash away from the house. Take it somewhere else to throw it out. (They had that weird burner oven in the back. Was it used to burn their trash? I had caught them throwing bags of trash in the dumpster.)

What to do if you think your neighbors are a meth house:

- Don't take matters into your own hands.
- Don't confront the neighbors.
- Report it to the police.

So, technically, I should report them to the police. But, were they really cooking meth? Just because they got a lot of deliveries and were reclusive, didn't mean they were doing anything illegal. And like the police hadn't already been here two times this week. Why not make it three? I could share my suspicions and then wait for them to look at me like I was crazy.

"Bojangles. Am I crazy?" I asked.

Bojangles licked my hand.

Just for good measure (and reassurance that I was not, in fact, crazy), I also checked out the page "Maybe It's A Grow House".

Common Signs

- High electricity use (for grow lights) and lights on day and night. (I didn't have their electric bill, so I had no idea.)
- Chemicals such as fertilizers and pesticides. (Yup! I'd seen them buy it at Home Depot.)
- High moisture levels/ condensation on the windows. (I quickly checked with my binoculars, but couldn't see anything like that.)
- Mold growing on the inside and outside walls. (Ew, gross! But I hadn't seen any on the outside with my binoculars, so they were prrrobably okay inside.)

Neighborhood Watch

- Ventilation system to remove excess moisture. (Didn't know.)
- Strong, stinky smell. (Ugh, yes!)

And just for good measure, I also checked out "Maybe It's A Chop Shop". Sadly, there were also indicators on this page that applied to the Miltons.

- Presence of numerous car parts on the property. (Sorta)
- Multiple dismantled vehicles. (Did two count as multiple?)
- Equipment to dismantle cars or remove engines/transmissions from vehicles. (No idea.)
- Cutting tools, saws, welding equipment. to include welding rigs or torches. (No idea.)
- High fences. (For sure!)
- Late nighttime hours. (ALL. THE. TIME.)
- Large tarps to hide the vehicles. (Yes, but was it vehicles they were hiding?)
- Vehicles enter but don't come out. (Hadn't seen that, but I'd only been here a week.)
- Trailers leave with vehicle parts or sections of cut-up pieces. (I hadn't seen a trailer there…yet.)

All the signs pointed to criminal behavior.

Chapter 13

From Now On, I Would Make Better Choices

Bojangles and I slept in the master bedroom bed, with the curtains drawn and white noise machine blasting, in my attempt to sleep instead of spy. Why should I even care? I was only visiting and once I left, I wouldn't have to think of the Miltons or this visit ever again.

Desperately needing to shake off the unsettled feeling that I had stumbled on some nefarious neighborhood crime ring, I took a pill. Then I settled down with the dog snuggled into the small of my back and went to sleep.

Sleeping under the influence of the medicine this time was no different than the last few times. My dreams were filled with crazy, illogical scenes of being trapped in the Milton's yard while looking for Bojangles and being chased by Mildred. The dream was just a weird variation of the other "prescription dreams" I'd had.

By the time I woke up at the usual hour of 2 a.m., I was in a cold sweat. The sheets were tangled, a byproduct of my thrashing around. I considered going to the front window and taking a look. No. Tonight would be different. Tonight I would make better choices. Instead of automatically heading into the living room and settling into the chair by the window, I would force myself to stay in bed and go back to sleep.

I would not go crazy. I would not overthink anything. Two more days and I could get out of this odd neighborhood that seemed to be an alternate universe.

Still feeling shaken up from the dream, I worked on some cognitive shuffling exercises instead of feeding my overactive imagination so I would not be paranoid.

SLEEP.

Sit, stand, silent, spy.

Live, laugh, love, look.

Eye, ear, elevate, elephant.

Echo, earwig, eat, end.

Pry, pray, preach, proof.

The exercise wasn't helping much. I stared up into the void of the pitch black room. The research I'd done before bed popped up in my mind and I allowed myself to settle in and think about it—examine it, if you will.

Security, blocked windows, tarps, deliveries, weird hours. Enough to suspect something illegal, but not enough to go to the police with. Heck, the police had already been here several times. If they didn't find anything to investigate further, then I should just leave it alone.

Although relaxing wasn't enjoyable anymore, that was what I was determined to do. Tomorrow I would take it easy, avoid any drama or supposed drama seen from the front window, and spend quality time with Bojangles before I left the next day. It was simple enough and I committed myself to doing just that.

Sally Johnson

* * *

On Friday, I watched the progress of my grocery delivery on live updates provided by the app. That's how bored I was. But, once I got the groceries, I was going to make some tacos for lunch and hang out with Annie. It was literally the highlight of my social calendar since I'd been at my uncle's. I was that pathetic. And my favorite pastime had become spying on the neighbors. I had sunk to depths of moral gray areas I'd never visited before.

Only two more days and my time here would be done. I'd be back at my apartment, probably just as bored, but away from the crazy neighbors across the street. I could visit with my friends and families and hear about the wedding and get caught up on workplace gossip. Honestly, I looked forward to it. Although I would miss Bojangles and the super comfy chair.

My phone flashed a notice that it was at seven percent, the battery was on yellow, and was well into the power-saving mode. As I went to plug it in, a notification popped up that my food delivery was here. So instead of plugging it in, I slipped it into my pocket and opened the door.

It was embarrassing to admit how excited I was just to talk to the delivery person. Or maybe I was just that excited about tacos for lunch. I really was going stir-crazy.

At the sound of a car door slamming, Bojangles went into barking mode. I peeked out the side window to see not only the delivery girl walking toward the house with two bags, but that the Miltons had just pulled into their driveway.

"Thank you," I said to the delivery girl as I opened the door and reached for the bags. The handles were twisted and one bag tipped forward, spilling out several cans and a bag of lettuce.

"Sorry! I'm sorry!" she said, and reached down to gather up the groceries.

I stepped onto the porch to offer my help. I was desperately looking forward to tacos and didn't want anything ruining lunch. I definitely couldn't enjoy tacos without RO-TEL tomatoes with chilis, and the can was about to fall off the edge of the step.

To my horror, Bojangles ran out the door.

"Bojangles!" I yelled. He didn't stop. He didn't even acknowledge me.

"Bojangles!" I yelled, with more authority.

It didn't work; he didn't care. Bojangles was effectively deaf to my command. He was on a mission–what it was, I didn't know. I wasn't sure if *he* knew what his mission was. But whatever it was, he was making a beeline to the neighbors' yard–the evil neighbors' yard.

No! No! No! Not *that* yard!

The delivery girl still stood frozen, still holding the head of lettuce but watching Bojangles' escape. I took off after him, slamming the door behind me.

"Sorry," I yelled over my shoulder. "I've got to get my dog. Just leave everything there. I'll pick it up after."

I realized I hadn't slipped my shoes on as my feet hit the gravelly, uneven road. "Ouch!" I exclaimed to no one. But that didn't matter because I had to catch that dog, so I tried to ignore it. I couldn't. I paused briefly to sweep my hand over the sole of my foot to brush away a stone that dug into my skin. By now Bojangles had run across the street (without bothering to look both ways) and toward the Milton's bushes. He stopped at a rose bush and began digging, kicking dirt behind his back paws. The bushes were barely planted, so the fresh, soft soil came up without much effort.

No! Not the rose bushes! Mildred would be at my front door–again–accusing me of something. How in just a few short days, had the situation changed to seem like I was harassing her? Although I *was* guilty of spying on her, I was completely innocent of harassing her.

But my dog, digging up the neighbor's landscaping, might be breaking some law. Could be even an obscure law. But if Bojangles was legitimately causing property damage, I would be held responsible. And Mildred would most definitely want to prosecute to the fullest extent of the law.

I was done! Once I got Bojangles back, I was out. I would close the curtains and return the chair to where it belonged and mind my own business. Neighbors coming home in the middle of the night. So what? Neighbors loading and unloading the car in the middle of the night? Who cared? Neighbors possibly being involved in illegal activities? Let the police deal with it. I was going to keep my head down and wait out my time here until Uncle Larry's return.

As I reached the edge of their lawn, Mildred rushed out of the front gate, scooped up Bojangles and ran through the side gate next to the garage.

Mildred stole Bojangles!

In a moment of bravado, I marched up to the front gate, grabbed a stick and rang the doorbell.

If she didn't answer the door, I was calling the cops.

My heart thudded in my throat. After waiting and listening for a few seconds, I didn't hear any movement inside. I grabbed my phone from my back pocket at the exact moment it started ringing. When I answered, Larry started talking before I could say hello.

"Isla? What's going on? Is Bojangles with you? I got a notification from his GPS that he's outside his–"

I cut him off. "I'm on it!"

"Where–" The line went dead.

Chapter 14

What Nightmares Are Made Of

C rap!
I shook my phone. "Larry? Larry?! Are you there?"

Was there something weird with the reception here? A pocket of no reception? Or–I glanced at my phone–a dead battery.

Double crap!

I put my phone away and tried the bell one more time–in case they somehow missed it or ignored it.

Nothing.

I tried the handle; it was locked. No surprise there. There was just dead silence.

That probably wasn't the best analogy– didn't want Bojangles to end up dead. Or me.

Where did she take Bojangles? I had to find him. I hurried to the wooden gate at the north end of the property–the site of the first altercation–and tried that gate. It was also locked. I tried to look over the top, but wasn't able to see anything. I settled for looking through the cracks of the slats. I couldn't see much of anything. I forced myself to stop and just listen. Maybe I could hear something, or someone, or Bojangles.

Nothing. Just the crickets and the passing traffic off in the distance.

I resumed my search. I went to the gate that Mildred had gone through and tried the handle. It was unlocked. And it opened!

With caution, I stepped through the gate. What if there was a motion-detection sensor that would trigger an alarm? All sorts of possibilities popped into my head with every step I took into forbidden territory.

I reached the corner of the house, which provided a full view of the backyard–and the stone oven thing. It really did look like an outdoor oven. Like one of those brick-oven-pizza-cooking kind, but this was much more Neanderthalic.

I approached it because 1) it wasn't smoking and 2) I wanted to get a better look at it and 3) I wanted to be sure Bojangles wasn't stuffed into it. Rocks of all different shapes and sizes were set into thick concrete. The shape was asymmetrical and gave the vibes of poor workmanship–definitely a DIY fail.

I reached out and ran my fingers over the rough stones. They were cool, further reassuring me it wasn't preheating.

Bark!

It was faint, but definitely a dog.

Bojangles?

I spun around toward the house and saw the bulkhead doors were open–the portal to the basement. No! Not the basement! Had Mildred taken Bojangles down there? I shivered as memories of my grandma's house sprang to mind. I stood at the edge of the open, rusty, metal door and stared into the void. The podcast about Hacksaw Harry made me hesitant to go there. And the bone Bojangles brought home fueled my hesitation.

The five steps leading into the basement had the same primitive feel of the backyard oven, with the uneven rocks and the thick concrete. Slowly, I placed my foot on the first step. Then the next and the next, until I stood on the packed, dirt floor. I forced myself to breathe slowly and fight the panic rising in my throat. I hated basements! The air was slightly cooler and the small area had a damp, earthy smell combined with a strong, fetid smell. A dark piece of tapestry-like fabric that I hadn't noticed before hung over the entrance. Was this the last warning to go away before entering a place of no return?

Carefully, I swept the heavy fabric aside.

A putrid smell punched me in the face. It was like something I had never smelled before–a combination of my grandma's musty basement, a crazy cat lady's house saturated with urine and a fridge that had died and was full of now-rotten meat.

I covered my nose and mouth with the neckline of my shirt and pressed my hand tight against it to create a makeshift mask. I swallowed down the saliva that had pooled in my mouth, threatening the dry heaves. I took a few tentative steps forward, but realized immediately it was impossible to see anything without lights. The battery on my phone was dead, so I couldn't use the flashlight. Even if I could find the light switch, did I dare turn it on?

I needed to turn back.

Some noise caught my attention and I froze, straining to listen. Was it Mildred and Glen? Bojangles? Had they trapped him in here and left him all alone? The poor baby would be so scared! Never mind the overwhelming stench that gave off predator-like smells. What kind of animal, or animals, could produce such a potent odor?

I couldn't make out the sound. Was it a conversation? Murmurs? Movement? A hum?

A few steps in and I struggled to make out the way. As my eyes grew accustomed to the dark, I could distinguish some dark outlines, but nothing more.

"You shouldn't have done that!" Glen's voice came from behind me, by the open door.

I froze, pressing my body against the closest, concrete wall, stumbling over something on the floor. I reached out to steady myself, but only felt what I guessed were boxes. I squatted down low, hoping if they came in they wouldn't see me.

"What else was I supposed to do? Let that dog dig up the rose bushes? They haven't been planted long enough," Mildred snapped.

"Well, no," Glen said. "But you could talk to her."

"I have talked to her and it hasn't done any good. She keeps snooping."

"I don't think she's doing it to provoke you," he said.

"Then why is she doing it?" Mildred hissed. "She suspects something."

Yes! I did suspect SOMETHING, because she kept gravedigger's hours and just stole my dog!

"And you just made it ten times worse by grabbing the dog."

See, Glen got it! Why didn't Mildred get it?

"Well, what do you suggest I do, Glen?" Mildred's words were laced with anger. "Since you've handled the situation so well so far."

"You could start by returning the dog. Bring it over and say it got lost in the yard."

Yes! Return Bojangles! Then I could leave this nasty-weird basement and go home.

"And then what?" Mildred asked.

"Nothing. Leave it at that. Walk away."

"But she saw me take the dog back here. She might've already called the police," Mildred said.

Which is exactly what I *should've* done.

"Then take it back immediately," Glen said.

"What if she doesn't answer?"

Did she know I was in her basement as she spoke?

"Leave it in the yard," Glen said.

"Just drop it over the fence?"

Yes! Yes! Please!

Glen coughed. Which made me want to cough. The air down here was so thick with humidity and rankness, I couldn't wait to get out and breathe in fresh air. As soon as they were gone, I was getting out, sneaking back to my uncle's house and calling the police for real.

Slam!

The space went pitch black.

No! No! No! No!

They had shut the door!

Chapter 15

What Just Happened?

My mind raced to process what just happened.

Yes, they had shut the door.

I immediately turned back. Maybe I could get out. Even if they were in the yard and saw me, it'd be better than being stuck in their nasty disgusting barf-bag nightmare world of a basement.

The situation could be worse. They could've locked the door.

Click!

I heard the slide of metal.

Uh-oh!

They had locked the door!

I was locked in! I. Was. Locked. In!

My breaths came fast. The disgusting air overcame me; I finally gave into the waves of nausea and ended up retching off to the side.

It's okay. It's okay. It's okay.

I wiped my mouth with the back of my hand and then pulled my shirt back up.

I forced myself to focus, creating a plan to get out of this situation before I went into a full-on panic attack.

I went back through the thick fabric blocking the door frame. There was a crack of light coming through where the two doors met. I tried the door; it didn't budge. If they had used a padlock, my attempts at escape would be completely futile.

I considered banging on the door, but I didn't really want them to find me in their basement. They'd probably accuse me of trespassing, which, I guess, technically was true. I'd keep the banging-on-the-door option as a last resort.

In a Hail Mary attempt to squeeze one last ounce of battery out of it, I tried my phone. I needed to call 911. I pushed the power button and the screen lit up! Yes! Maybe I could be rescued. With my hope renewed, I–

The screen went black, dousing my hopes of rescue.

I tried again, but nothing happened. And once again to see I could at least get the flashlight to turn on, even if just for a split second.

My phone was completely dead.

I stood still, waiting for my eyes to adjust to the darkness. But after a few minutes, I gave up. They must've blocked off the windows. Larry had a light in his, but it turned on by a switch at the top of the stairs. Perhaps there were lights hanging in their ceiling. My grandmother had those long tube ones. She'd also had spiders in her rafters. If I reached up into the dark unknown, would I touch a spider?

My other option was to remain here paralyzed with fear and die, never to be found again.

I reached up. I didn't touch anything. Not wood, not ceiling, not spider webs. I must've been too short to touch the ceiling.

But I discovered if I reached my arms out, I could touch both sides of the cool, rough concrete wall. It was a very narrow path, making me think the basement was divided into rooms. But where were the windows? Surely there had to be windows. I tried to picture where the windows were in my uncle's basement, but couldn't recall because I hadn't paid attention. Why would I? I didn't think in my wildest dreams (or nightmares) that I'd get locked in a basement.

Windows were beside the point. I needed to find another way out of here. Maybe they had a door in the basement that led to their kitchen upstairs, like what Larry had. Could I find it in this pitch black space that was most likely filled with hazards piled high along the way? I had to try.

With my hand over my nose, I stumbled forward. I visualized Larry's basement and tried to situate where I was in relation to what I remembered of his basement.

I thought I could hear the noise again. Murmurs. Or voices. It didn't have the rhythm of a conversation or of music. It could possibly be fans. It didn't sound like saws disassembling cars. Maybe it was the hum of homemade cookers hooked up and making meth. I could potentially be walking myself straight into their meth lab. If the Miltons were in there, would they kill to keep their secret?

It was slow going. I tripped on an unknown and unseen object and slammed my toe into something hard. I bit my lip to stop myself from crying out in pain. I felt some sort of foam handle. Possibly exercise equipment? Whatever it was, it hurt! Bare feet were not proper foot protection when stumbling around in the dark of a stranger's dungeon of a basement.

As I came to a corner, I used my left arm to reach out, hoping to find the opposite wall to steady myself, but there was nothing. With my right hand as a guide, I slowly made my way around to the right, closer and closer to the noise.

My fingers touched something cool and I wrapped my hand around a metal knob. Was this a door leading upstairs? I slowly turned it to see if it was unlocked. It moved! Since it was probably my best chance of escape at the moment, I opened it and felt my way through the frame.

The noise was louder–loud enough that I wished I had ear plugs. It sounded like a loud warehouse fan or ventilation system. And the stench–it was so much more pungent. And not just urine. But poop.

The floor felt different. I was no longer on the cool dirt or concrete, but something almost scratchy, like old, crusty carpet. I stepped slowly, in case there was anything sharp or possibly dead underfoot. As I put my weight on it, it felt somewhat spongey. Maybe shag carpeting.

My right hand ran up the sides of the door and I felt something!

Soft, but solid. Hair? Fur? A creepy doll or clown?

And then metal. Was there a carpet hanging over a metal frame?

Then it moved!

I yanked my hand away and shrunk against the left side of the door frame. What was that? A huge tarantula spider? A shrunken head? Taxidermy? *A person?!*

Holy crap! Were they human traffickers?

Was that their secret?

The horrible smell would make sense if they were hiding people in their basement.

"Hello?" I said in a tenuous voice. The loud fans drowned out my words.

There had to be something in here. Something responsible for the smell.

Slowly, I patted the wooden frame of the door with my left hand. I was afraid of spiders, splinters and whatever else I had touched with my other hand. But I was also afraid of dying, so I kept looking for an escape.

I finally felt a small, smooth, cool switch.

Click. I flipped it up.

A single, dim bulb hanging in the middle of a large room lit up.

The walls were lined with dark, black foam and stacked cages filled the room. At first I wasn't sure what I was looking at. Monsters. Hairy, monsters.

As my eyes adjusted to the lights, I realized what I was looking at.

They weren't monsters!

They were dogs!

Chapter 16
I Had To Get Out!

The room was full of dogs!

They were smelly, some of their coats overgrown and matted and they were living in their own filth.

The poor babies!

The illuminated room created a frenzy of movement and sound. As I moved closer to the cages, I could see more and more dogs. There was a burst of barking, which I could only hear close up because the noise of the huge fan drowned out a lot of the sound.

How long had they been down here, living in these wretched, disgusting conditions without sunlight, ventilation and proper sanitation? I *had* to save them.

Were the Miltons experimenting on them?

Were they animal hoarders too? An illegal puppy mill? In a dog-fighting ring and collecting dogs as bait?

Everything suddenly made sense. The smell, the noise, the crates. They were hiding dogs. And not just two or three. I spun around and tried to count the dog crates, some two or three high, stacked on top of each other. My guesstimate was twenty dogs.

Now that I knew their secret, escaping became more urgent. I not only had to get out, but I had to save these poor, abused dogs.

The best plan I could come up with was to go back the way I came. Then I'd force the bulkhead doors open.

If that didn't work, I'd bang on the door. Hopefully that would create enough of a commotion that they'd come let me out. I could play dumb and say I thought Bojangles ran in there and I was trying to get him. Or, I could figure it out as I went along and just focus on getting out of the basement first.

If I propped open the door to the animal "prison", a little bit of light shone into the hall. But the light only illuminated it so far and then it faded into blackness again. But I was out of options. I hurriedly retraced my steps, but hit my knee on something sharp as I turned the corner. I reached down and pressed on my knee and when I pulled my hand away, it was wet. I must've been bleeding. It sure stung a lot. Was I going to need a Tetanus shot? The germs in this basement had to be crazy bad.

I stumbled along, virtually blind. When my fingertips finally touched the rough texture of the heavy fabric, I released the breath I'd been holding and flung the cloth aside. Seeing the tiny strip of light between the doors renewed my hope of escape. I pushed on it again, but the door still didn't budge. I stepped down two steps, tucked my head and then rushed it. Pain shot through my shoulder and down my back. That wasn't going to work and I didn't need to shatter any bones trying. Which left banging and screaming.

"HELP! HELP ME!" I screamed. "I'M IN HERE!" I

yelled over and over until I was hoarse. In between screams, I pounded on the doors with my fists. Someone had to hear me. Someone, anyone, even if it was Mildred and Glen.

I had no idea how long I had been down there screaming and pounding. My head hurt, my shoulder hurt, my eyes hurt and I started to lose hope. I was going to die down here and when Mildred and Glen found me, I'd be burned in that outside oven. They'd spread my ashes among the rose bushes, mixed in with fertilizer and horse manure and my remains would never be found.

I sat on the uneven, stone steps and gave into despair. Tears filled my eyes and spilled over onto my cheeks and I didn't bother to wipe them away. My hands had to be so filthy from everything I had touched down here. I didn't need to add an eye infection to the lock jaw/asphyxiation/starvation combination of ways I could die.

"What's down there?" I heard someone say outside. Glen? Mildred? A neighbor? Had someone heard my screams for help and come to investigate?

"Nothing," snapped a voice I recognized–Mildred.

I pounded on the doors. "I'm in here! Please! Help me!"

"Is someone locked in there?" It was a male voice that didn't sound like Glen.

"No," Glen said. "We just have–"

"I'm in here," I screamed and pounded again.

"Open the door, please," the man instructed.

With the slide of metal, light flooded my prison. I squinted against the sunshine.

"WHY ARE YOU IN THERE?" Mildred yelled at me.

"We weren't keeping her hostage," Glen said.

I struggled to focus my eyes as the sun blinded me, but I

was never more happy to be blinded by the light than at that moment.

Someone reached down and offered me a hand. "Ma'am. Are you okay? What are you doing in there?"

With his support, I climbed out of the basement and was shocked at what came into focus. The backyard was filled with police officers.

"I'm, uh..." I rasped, blinking rapidly. "I got locked in. I'm looking for my dog."

"SHE WAS TRESPASSING!" Mildred screamed.

My heart beat wildly. Were they going to arrest me for trespassing?

"No, no," I protested, trying to catch my breath. "They took my dog."

"Did you find your dog?" the officer asked.

I shook my head. I couldn't think and I was so thirsty.

Mildred hurled more accusations about trespassing. Was I in trouble?

"I need to sit," I said and sunk onto the edge of the bulkhead frame.

"Did you find your dog?" the officer repeated.

"No." Off to my left, Mildred continued her verbal assault.

"Could I get some water?" I asked.

"Could you get her some water?" the cop asked. An officer at the back peeled off from the group and walked away from where we were. He returned quickly with a bottle of water.

I looked closer and realized it was Officer Nettles. *Nettles?* I exhaled; I felt safe with him taking care of me.

"Thank you," I said. After a long gulp, I said, "She took Bojangles." I directed my comments to Officer Nettles.

"Bo who?" the first cop said.

"Bojangles. My dog. Mildred snatched him up and ran into this side of the yard. I followed her and ended up getting locked in."

"Did she go in there?" the cop asked, pointing to the basement.

"I don't know," I said as tears welled up in my eyes. "They weren't in the yard and I couldn't see them anywhere, but this door was open. I had to find him! I had to! So I went down there to look and the door shut!"

Officer Nettles squatted down beside me and patted my knee. Then he turned toward the couple. "Do you have her dog?"

"He's in the house," Mildred stuttered as she answered. "For safekeeping. Because he ran away. I was going to bring him back. I didn't know if she was home."

I sniffled and wiped my nose with my sleeve. "They have dogs," I blurted out and pointed at the deep, dark cavern. "They have a ton of neglected dogs down there."

"No we don't. We don't have dogs," Mildred snapped.

I nodded emphatically. "They do. They have dogs. That's why it smells so bad."

Officer Nettles looked to another officer as if to pass the responsibility on to a superior.

"Do you have dogs down there?" the first officer asked.

"We don't have dogs," Mildred repeated.

"Are there any more people in there? Do you have more hostages?" The other cop directed his questions to the couple.

"Hostages? She's not a hostage!" Mildred said, her arm extended in my direction. "She was trespassing!"

The cop shifted his focus to me. "Are there more hostages down there?"

"I didn't see people, but I don't know for sure."

Mildred gesticulated with her hands. "She wasn't a hostage! She snuck down there! She trespassed!"

"And you locked her in." the officer supplied.

Glen shook his head. "No. She–"

"I didn't lock myself in," I matched Mildred's accusatory tone. "Someone shut the door from the outside!"

"We didn't know she was in there!" Mildred said, her voice rising. "She was trespassing!"

"Mind if we search your property?" the officer asked.

"Yes, we mind. You're going to need a search warrant," Glen answered.

"We can do that. And we're also placing you under arrest."

Chapter 17
What They Were Hiding

O fficer Nettles escorted me to the ambulance and left me in the care of an EMT. "I'll be back soon to take your statement."

They wrapped a blanket around me and I sat in the back of the ambulance while they checked me out. The cut on my knee didn't need stitches (yay!) and I didn't need a Tetanus shot (double yay!). My hands were cleaned up and the abrasions were treated and I was told to expect some bruising. The EMT cleared me and suggested I sit on a bench at the side of the driveway until Officer Nettles came to talk to me. From where I sat, I had a direct sightline of Mildred and Glen sitting in the back of separate police cars. I couldn't see their expressions, but took comfort from having witnessed them be led away in handcuffs and seeing them detained.

There was a lot of waiting on the search warrant. Yellow crime scene tape was stretched across the perimeter of the property. More police cars rolled up, as well as another animal control truck, and state troopers. Their vehicles choked up the street.

Neighborhood Watch

Once the search warrant was issued and executed, there was a flurry of activity. I watched from afar as officers entered the house through the front door. Although I couldn't see it, I heard as the officers entered the basement.

My stomach roiled as I watched cage after cage, crate after crate of animals loaded into the trucks. Bojangles could've ended up in one of those cages.

When Officer Nettles returned, he had Bojangles in his arms. "I believe he belongs to you." Bojangles leapt from Officer Nettles arms and into mine. He greeted me with an onslaught of wet kisses on my lips as he wiggled with excitement. It didn't bother me at all.

I squeezed him tight, trying to contain him. I couldn't let him run off again. "Where was he?" I asked.

He frowned. "Locked in a bathroom."

"You poor baby," I said. "You're going to be okay." Did dogs experience PTSD? Would he be able to forget this horrible experience as I hoped to be able to?

Thankfully, Officer Nettles was also the one who questioned me and took down my statement. I explained the whole story, Bojangles' escape, searching for him, getting locked in the basement and my discovery. He didn't make me feel crazy, or that I imagined the whole thing. He just quietly wrote everything down.

"What's going to happen to them?" I asked and nodded to Glen and Mildred who were still in the police cars.

"They'll more than likely be arrested and be charged with kidnapping and animal cruelty. There could be more charges depending on what is found during the search."

"Kidnapping?" I asked. "But they didn't take me anywhere or hold me for ransom."

"You were unlawfully detained by them. There doesn't need to be a ransom."

Huh.

"How did you find me?" I asked, suddenly wondering about my rescue.

"Do you know Annie?"

Annie! I nodded.

"She was cleaning next door," he motioned to the house beside the Milton's, "and thought she heard yelling coming from this yard. She's over there talking to the detectives."

"She's here?" I asked, looking around. All I saw was police lights, officers, and official-looking people. They were everywhere. As I scanned the yard, I didn't see Annie.

"I'll send her over when she's done," he said. I didn't want him to leave me alone, but I had no reason to ask him to stay.

As I watched Officer Nettles weave through the maze of people to the other side of the yard, I was able to see where he pointed to. If I stood, I could see better, but I was too exhausted and my legs felt wobbly. I rested my head in my hands and closed my eyes. The tug of a headache pulled at my temple and the heaviness of exhaustion overwhelmed me.

"Isla!" A voice called out.

I opened my eyes as a familiar figure rushed up to me. "Isla! Isla!"

"Annie!"

Annie hugged me. "Are you okay?"

"I'm so glad you're here! You saved me," I managed. My eyes burned as I blinked back tears.

She shrugged. "Well, I called the cops."

"I thought I was going to die in their basement!" I broke down crying.

She hugged me and patted my back. "I'm glad I heard

you," she said when we separated after a moment. "Honestly, I felt stupid when I called."

I looked from Annie to the house and then back to Annie. "I'm glad too." Because if she hadn't heard me, how long would I have been in there? Larry might've eventually missed me, but, again, it might've taken hours before he realized something was wrong.

"What was down there?" Annie asked.

"Dogs. They're hiding a roomful of dogs."

"Like as pets or...?"

"I couldn't tell."

"What do you think they were doing with all those animals?"

I shook my head. "I think it was something evil.

* * *

Eventually I was cleared to go. I headed home clutching several business cards with the event number written on the back, Bojangles in my arms and Annie by my side.

Once inside, Annie suggested I relax. "Do you still want to make dinner, or should I order pizza?" she asked. It wasn't until she mentioned pizza that I remembered the tacos and realized how famished I was. And with the day I'd had, I wouldn't be cooking.

She gathered the groceries that were abandoned by the front door before joining me in the living room. We watched out the front window as we waited for the pizza to be delivered.

Another police truck arrived and parked in front of the Miltons, effectively blocking our front-row view of the crime scene unfolding. Even with the help of my binoculars, I couldn't get the right angle to see around the vehicles.

"This is sort of surreal, you know?" Annie said. "It's like watching a scene in a movie."

I nodded. "Except we're in it."

Annie craned her neck as she stood in front of the window. "I hope the pizza person can make it to the driveway."

"Me too. I'm starving."

Despite the congestion of official vehicles and having some of the street being taped off, the delivery person managed to get our precious food to the house with only minor inconveniences. He was thanked profusely and sent off with a generous tip.

After eating, I felt better and could think clearer. I plugged in my phone and a cascade of messages lit up my screen—all from Larry.

Larry: Bojangles' GPS location says he's not at home. Are you guys on a walk? Did his collar fall off? Is the tracker battery low?

Larry: I just checked again. He's still not home. Is he with you?

Larry: Isla, where are you? Call me.

Larry: Are you okay?

Larry: Is something wrong?

Larry: I'm officially worried.

Larry: Annie texted me. She's looking for you.

Larry: She says you're not home but there's groceries on the porch. Should I call the police?

Larry: Isla?

Larry: Text me as soon as you get this. I don't care what time it is.

As my fingers hovered over my screen, poised to text a

response, I struggled to think of the words. I...it was so much to explain.

My phone rang and Larry's name popped up on my screen.

"Hello?" I said. Suddenly I was tired. My eyes felt heavy and for the first time all week, I genuinely wanted to sleep.

"Isla? Are you okay? What is going on?" Larry was frantic.

"I'm okay. I'm okay!" I said.

"And Bojangles? Is he safe? Is he okay?" The frantic edge in his voice was more pronounced when he asked about his dog.

"Bojangles is safe. He's on my lap right now." He was curled up and it looked like he had an actual smile on his face. Petting him had kept me from completely freaking out.

"What's going on there?" Larry asked.

As I gave him the condensed version, I looked across the street at the active crime scene. Police lights lit up the neighborhood like a Christmas tree. Neighbors were outside rubbernecking, but for once, I didn't care to join. I didn't want to leave the safety of Larry's house.

"I can come home now. I'll take the next flight out," Larry said.

I considered his offer. "You'll only be home a day earlier; I'll survive." I was trying to play it cool because, what if Larry never trusted me again? "And Annie's going to stay here tonight." She had offered when we returned to the house, even though I had insisted I was fine. But she insisted I wasn't fine, so eventually I gave in and agreed to have her sleep in the guest room. "I really think it's okay."

"Are you sure?"

Larry reluctantly took my word for it, and we hung up

with the stipulation that if anything changed, I'd call him immediately.

Before going to bed, I took a long, hot shower. The stench of the Milton's basement clung to me–my clothes, my hair, my skin–and I needed to wash the smell and, ideally, the ordeal, off of me. By the time I stepped out of the shower, my skin was wrinkled and my eyes were heavy.

I couldn't wait to go to bed.

Once I was settled, with Bojangles by my side, I realized that I did feel better knowing Annie was across the hall. I set my phone on "DO NOT DISTURB" for the next twelve hours and turned out the lights.

I yawned as the exhaustion set in. It was like the burst of adrenaline that had kept me alive the last few hours ran out and I was about to crash. Now that Mildred and Glen were arrested and the cops had taken control of their house, I didn't have anything else to worry about. Mildred and Glen were behind a new set of bars.

Chapter 18

Breaking News

A phone call woke me in the morning. I lifted my head from the down pillow and grabbed it from the nightstand.

"Hello?" I said, not even trying to hide the sleep from my voice.

"I'm coming home." It was Larry and he sounded like he was walking quickly and out of breath.

I sat up. "What?"

"Have you turned on the news?" Larry asked.

I rubbed my eyes and cleared my throat. "No. Why?" I literally just woke up and never watched the news. Even if I did, my first priority was always coffee and once that kicked in, laying around the house being bored.

"Glen and Mildred are breaking news."

"I bet," I said as I rolled over. I put Larry on speaker and checked my texts. Twenty texts? *Twenty?*

The first one was from Annie saying she had to go, but would check in with me later. What time was it? My home screen read 11:38. I had slept over fourteen hours!

Three missed calls from Larry.

Five texts from my mom—

Larry interrupted my scrolling. "Did you hear me, Isla?"

"Sorry. What?"

"They found bones in the yard!"

"Bones?!" Really? I wasn't crazy! I flung off the sheets.

"Apparently the police are still out there excavating."

"Let me go check."

I scurried to the living room, with Bojangles at my heels, and whipped open the curtains of the front window. I was fully visible and I completely didn't care.

Vans with tall antennas lined the street. News reporters stood in front of cameras, filming their segments. I absolutely knew now was not a good time to check the mail.

"The news people are everywhere outside," I said. "It's a big story, huh?" I struggled to wrap my head around the reality.

"I had no idea psychopaths lived across the street from me," Larry said in a low voice, heavy with disbelief.

"Obviously no one did."

"It sounds like they are still in jail," Larry said.

I sure hoped so. I didn't want to be alone when the Miltons were released. Mildred would be back on the doorstep, beating down the door because she got arrested. Somehow it would be my fault. "What time do you get back?" I asked.

"About four. I'll grab an Uber when I land. Stay safe and see you in a few hours."

"Okay." I reassured Larry three more times we'd be okay (even though I wasn't completely confident) before we hung up. I didn't dare tempt fate and ask "what could go wrong?" I for sure wasn't going to do anything but lay low and stay inside today, just like my doctor had originally ordered.

Neighborhood Watch

For the first time all week, I sat down and watched TV. I flipped through the channels which confirmed what Larry had told me: all of the local news channels showed a picture of the Milton's house. The news ticker proclaimed *Breaking News!*

I paused on one channel that was broadcasting live. The man behind the news desk, Jim Shelligan, spoke. "We're going live to the scene where Penny Thomas is reporting. What have you found out, Penny?"

A woman with dark hair held a microphone and nodded at the camera. "Authorities are calling this a hoarding house of horrors. Neighbors in this quiet neighborhood are shocked today at the discovery of over thirty dogs hidden in the basement of this house located at three Chestnut Street. Homeowners Glen and Mildred Milton were arrested after a neighbor called the police and reported banging and yelling coming from the backyard. What authorities discovered was chilling."

They cut to a clip of Officer Nathan Nettles. Officer Nettles! I had all the feels. I smiled, happy to see him and my stomach flip-flopped in hopes to be able to see him again.

"Dispatch received reports of someone yelling at the residence of three Chestnut Street. Responding officers discovered a female in her mid-twenties locked in the basement. After obtaining a warrant, officers conducted a search of the house and property. They found a room in the basement where approximately thirty dogs were recovered. The dogs were in deplorable conditions and were transported by animal control to the local shelter where they will be treated."

The camera switched back to Penny. "Behind me you

can see investigators are digging up the yard, but have yet to comment on any findings."

The screen split and Jim from the studio appeared. "Penny, do we know why the couple had so many animals?"

"Thank you, Penny," Jim said, then looked directly at the camera. "This is a developing story. We'll keep you updated as more information is released."

I surfed the channels looking for new information, but all the news had the same story.

Head rest was thrown out the window for the day. I watched the news and Bojangles watched out the window and protected me with incessant barking. I was bombarded with calls from Larry, (he finally boarded the plane!), had a lengthy phone call with my mom, and a continuous stream of texting with Sierra and Lola. There was still a flow of news reporters making segments in front of the residence and knocking doors in attempts to interview neighbors and ask their reactions.

Anytime there was a knock on the door, I ignored it.

Larry called just over an hour later. "They were in a dogfighting ring!" He once again sounded like he was on the move. In the background, I could hear a voice announcing a gate change—Larry must've just landed.

My mouth fell open and it felt like the air got sucked out of my lungs. "The Miltons? How do you know?" Between naps, I constantly checked the news and refreshed my Google search bar on my phone. Details unfolded slowly throughout the day, but I hadn't heard anything as shocking as that.

"My neighbor was contacted by the cops. They found his dog's tags in the yard. Their dog has been missing for months. It had been buried under a rose bush."

The planting! The fertilizer! The smell! Oh, my gosh!

They were burying animals! "Were you able to find anything else out?"

The news had supplied images of the living conditions both on the main floor and in the basement. The Miltons were, indeed, hoarders. Their house was jam-packed with stuff that choked out the living space in the house, leaving the owners with only pathways through the house.

But the information only trickled out. I needed to know what had *really* been going on.

"They found over thirty dogs alive. They were kept in a room that had been soundproofed. There was foam insulation and loud fans. They also found muzzles."

At least the dogs were still alive. Now they could be treated and hopefully adopted into a fur-ever home. "How did cops figure out they were involved with dogfighting?" The thought sickened me. How could someone do that to defenseless animals? Keeping them caged was bad enough, but forcing them to fight? Was that why Mildred grabbed Bojangles? I had to shut the thoughts down quickly; it was too horrible to think about.

"There were treadmills in the basement."

"Which, by the looks of it, the Miltons didn't use. But how is it connected?"

"It tipped the police off to why they had so many dogs. Apparently treadmills are used to train the dogs. I don't really know."

Pieces started clicking into place. "They'd move dogs at night. That's what I was seeing."

"That'd be my guess."

"How did nobody know?" It was more of a rhetorical question.

"They've been my neighbors for over ten years and they

managed to keep their double life secret," Larry said. I could hear the shock in his voice–what a bombshell.

I thought about it for a minute. "I guess it goes to show, how well does anyone know their neighbors?"

"Apparently not very well." He paused. "My Uber's here; I'll see you soon."

Larry arrived about an hour later. The scene across the street was still actively being used for news updates. After he and Bojangles reunited through multiple licks and hugs, Larry went out and talked to the news crews. He even went on camera and shared his surprise about discovering what the neighbors were hiding.

He proceeded to visit all his neighbors in the cul-de-sac to glean more information. When he returned, he didn't have any new details and seemed perplexed.

He sat in the gray chair and sighed loudly. Bojangles jumped off my lap and onto his, as if to comfort him. "I thought my neighborhood was safe, only to find out my neighbors were criminals. How did I miss that?"

"Sounds like you need to create a neighborhood watch," I suggested.

"And you should be president," Larry said.

Two Months Later

Memories hit me as soon as we entered Larry's house—the scent of lemons; the skittering of Bojangles' paws on the hardwood floor. I reminded myself to breathe and focus on the moment and not the memories.

"Someone is looking forward to seeing you again," Larry said as he set my suitcase down.

Of course, I knew he meant Bojangles. Funny enough, I had missed my nap buddy. That was one thing I looked forward to coming back to visit Uncle Larry's.

"Bojangles!" I said, genuinely happy to see him. I scooped him up and snuggled him in my arms. He licked my lips and this time, I actually didn't mind it.

"There are blackout curtains in the guest room for you," Larry said and rolled my carry-on down the hall. "I'll put this in there."

"Thank you," I said.

"How is the concussion?" Larry asked when he returned from the bedroom. We went and sat in the front room. I claimed the comfy chair, while Larry sat in the uncomfortable, gray armchair.

The time at his house had set my recovery back a week. Too much "excitement" and not enough head rest–I had played detective and now I had to pay. It was all my fault. "I still have a couple of months of head rest. It's still boring. My life isn't as exciting as it was here."

Larry squinted his eyes in suspicion. "Oh, yeah?"

"Okay, I PROMISE I'm done with THAT sort of excitement in my life. Head rest is just not as fun without Bojangles," I said and kissed him on top of his head. Bojangles rewarded me with a lick on the lips.

"He missed you," Larry said.

I didn't believe it. "He couldn't have gotten that attached to me in six days."

"A lot can happen in six days, as we saw."

I shrugged. "True."

Larry raised his eyebrows. "You've been following the story, right?"

Of course! I stalked the news. And Larry sent me texts with updates as more details emerged.

After I'd left, the story unfolded over the next couple of days. The late-night trips the Miltons took were used to catch strays or steal neighborhood pets. Other times, they picked up free pets offered on social media sale sites. Some animals were used as bait animals, and bigger animals were trained for fights.

The police dug up all of the rose bushes and discovered a pet cemetery. The fertilizer and manure were used to mask the smell of dead animals. As animals passed away from neglect, injuries or fights, they were buried around the yard under the roses.

The arrest of the Miltons led to the discovery of others

involved in the ring and led to more arrests and seizure of animals.

"I still talk to the police about the case," I said. Officer Nettles had been one of my points of contact and to be honest, I wasn't terribly sad about that. He was not only easy on the eyes, but he was easy to talk to. Another point of contact I spoke to while the state built their case had been Sylvia at Victim & Witness Services. But she wasn't as fun to talk to.

"About yourself or the case?"

I blushed. Somehow, he knew.

"So, do you know any more than the news is reporting about your kidnapping?" Larry asked. He leaned forward as if I had more details to dish.

Although I'd corrected Larry many times, he still referred to the situation as kidnapping. According to Officer Nettles, it technically hadn't been kidnapping or even false imprisonment, but criminal negligence.

Bojangles jumped into my lap. "Some, but not everything," I said. In two days, I'd be privy to all the details as I was going to be the "star" witness (okay, that's an exaggeration of my importance) in the court case against the Miltons. I shared with him what I knew and we discussed the details for almost a half hour.

Larry checked his phone just as the doorbell chimed. Right on cue, Bojangles started barking. "Someone else is looking forward to seeing you again," Larry said as he got up.

He opened the door and I heard a familiar voice. Officer Nathan Nettles.

Why was he here? He hadn't mentioned stopping by in our last conversation.

"Hey," I said when our eyes met. He was barely over the

threshold, wearing jeans and a light blue T-shirt. "I didn't recognize you with your clothes on."

His eyebrows raised and Larry coughed. I quickly realized my gaffe.

My cheeks burned. "I mean, out of your uniform."

It wasn't getting any better.

"You mean, in my street clothes," he offered.

I nodded. "Yes. That's exactly what I mean."

Although a man in uniform was easy on the eyes, Nathan in street clothes wasn't any less attractive.

After greeting Larry and being invited to sit on the hard-as-a-board couch, his attention turned to me.

"I knew you were in town and wanted to stop by. Did the DA's office call you?"

I shook my head. "I haven't gotten any calls today. What's going on?" It had to be big news if he came to deliver it personally.

Officer Nettles looked from me, to Larry and back at me again. "The Miltons took a plea deal."

I exhaled in a low *whoosh*. "I don't have to testify?" A plea had always been a possibility, so I was both surprised and not surprised. "They didn't want to gamble on a trial?" As I said the words, it felt like a literal weight lifted off my chest.

"The case has garnered a lot of attention and a lot of protests, especially from animal activists. I think the Miltons realized their odds were better taking the plea deal than chancing it in court."

"No amount of sentencing will suffice for the torture they inflicted on those animals," Larry said and hugged Bojangles. "They should be locked up for a long time. Long enough that they'd never come up for parole, live the rest of the days caged like the animals they'd hoarded, and eventually die in prison."

We all agreed.

"So the trial is over? Like, it's settled?" I asked.

"It's settled," Officer Nettles nodded. "You should hear from the DA's office soon. In fact, I'm surprised you haven't already."

The news felt weirdly surreal. Could it really be over just like that and everyone would just move on with their lives? For me, I was still working on forgetting the experience and moving forward with my life.

"Looks like your schedule has suddenly opened up," Larry said, looking from me to Officer Nettles.

I shrugged. "I'm left, once again, wondering what I should do with myself while I'm here."

"I can think of a few suggestions," Officer Nettles said, his eyebrows raised.

"Oh, yeah? Like what?" I said.

"How about grabbing lunch?" he asked with a smile.

Acknowledgments

As much as I would love to have my first draft be my last draft because it is absolute perfection, that is never the case. It requires much help from editors, beta readers, and those who have knowledge outside my expertise. There is no way Neighborhood Watch would be the book that it is without said help. I truly am grateful to all of those who helped me along the way.

Beta Readers: Sally Nelson, Audrey Morgan, Kristi Ericksson, Gretchen Stella

Concussion patient and "Head Rest" and survivor Megan Mettmann

Proofreader Extrordonaires Danielle Booker and Michelle Morgan

Retired LVMPD detective Mike Hope, who answered all my questions and made my story procedurally correct. And retired District Attorney Ron Bloxham for answering all my legal questions.

Made in the USA
Columbia, SC
07 April 2025